PENGUIN CANADA

THE PENGUIN BOOK OF CRIME STORIES
VOLUME II

PETER ROBINSON is the author of eighteen Inspector Banks novels, including his latest, *All the Colours of Darkness,* as well as two non-series books, *Caedmon's Song* and *No Cure for Love.* He has published two collections of short stories. His novels have been translated into over twenty languages, and he has won a number of international awards, including the MWA Edgar, the CWA Dagger in the Library, the Martin Beck Award from Sweden, the Danish Palle Rosenkrantz Award, and the French Grand Prix de Littérature Policière. He has also won five Crime Writers of Canada Arthur Ellis Awards.

In 2007 Robinson edited *The Penguin Book of Crime Stories,* which was published to great critical acclaim.

Peter Robinson lives in Toronto and in Richmond, North Yorkshire.

THE PENGUIN BOOK OF
CRIME STORIES

VOLUME II

SELECTED AND INTRODUCED BY

PETER
ROBINSON

PENGUIN
CANADA

PENGUIN CANADA

Published by the Penguin Group

Penguin Group (Canada), 90 Eglinton Avenue East, Suite 700, Toronto, Ontario, Canada
M4P 2Y3 (a division of Pearson Canada Inc.)

Penguin Group (USA) Inc., 375 Hudson Street, New York, New York 10014, U.S.A.
Penguin Books Ltd, 80 Strand, London WC2R 0RL, England
Penguin Ireland, 25 St Stephen's Green, Dublin 2, Ireland (a division of Penguin Books Ltd)
Penguin Group (Australia), 250 Camberwell Road, Camberwell, Victoria 3124, Australia
(a division of Pearson Australia Group Pty Ltd)
Penguin Books India Pvt Ltd, 11 Community Centre, Panchsheel Park,
New Delhi – 110 017, India
Penguin Group (NZ), 67 Apollo Drive, Rosedale, North Shore 0745, Auckland, New Zealand
(a division of Pearson New Zealand Ltd)
Penguin Books (South Africa) (Pty) Ltd, 24 Sturdee Avenue, Rosebank,
Johannesburg 2196, South Africa

Penguin Books Ltd, Registered Offices: 80 Strand, London WC2R 0RL, England

First published 2010

1 2 3 4 5 6 7 8 9 10 (WEB)

Introduction and selection copyright © Eastvale Enterprises, Inc., 2010
The Copyright Acknowledgments on pages 209–210 constitute
an extension of this copyright page.

Manufactured in Canada.

LIBRARY AND ARCHIVES CANADA CATALOGUING IN PUBLICATION

The Penguin book of crime stories : volume II / selected and introduced
by Peter Robinson.

ISBN 978-0-14-317234-5

1. Crime—Fiction. 2. Detective and mystery stories, Canadian (English).
3. Detective and mystery stories, American. 4. Detective and mystery
stories, English. 5. Canadian fiction (English). 6. American fiction.
7. English fiction. I. Robinson, Peter, 1950- II. Title.
PN6120.95.D45P463 2010   C813'.087208   C2009-907529-6

Visit the Penguin Group (Canada) website at **www.penguin.ca**

Special and corporate bulk purchase rates available; please see
www.penguin.ca/corporatesales or call 1-800-810-3104, ext. 2477 or 2474

THE PENGUIN BOOK OF

CRIME STORIES

VOLUME II

SELECTED AND INTRODUCED BY

PETER
ROBINSON

PENGUIN
CANADA

PENGUIN CANADA

Published by the Penguin Group

Penguin Group (Canada), 90 Eglinton Avenue East, Suite 700, Toronto, Ontario, Canada
M4P 2Y3 (a division of Pearson Canada Inc.)

Penguin Group (USA) Inc., 375 Hudson Street, New York, New York 10014, U.S.A.
Penguin Books Ltd, 80 Strand, London WC2R 0RL, England
Penguin Ireland, 25 St Stephen's Green, Dublin 2, Ireland (a division of Penguin Books Ltd)
Penguin Group (Australia), 250 Camberwell Road, Camberwell, Victoria 3124, Australia
(a division of Pearson Australia Group Pty Ltd)
Penguin Books India Pvt Ltd, 11 Community Centre, Panchsheel Park,
New Delhi – 110 017, India
Penguin Group (NZ), 67 Apollo Drive, Rosedale, North Shore 0745, Auckland, New Zealand
(a division of Pearson New Zealand Ltd)
Penguin Books (South Africa) (Pty) Ltd, 24 Sturdee Avenue, Rosebank,
Johannesburg 2196, South Africa

Penguin Books Ltd, Registered Offices: 80 Strand, London WC2R 0RL, England

First published 2010

1 2 3 4 5 6 7 8 9 10   (WEB)

Introduction and selection copyright © Eastvale Enterprises, Inc., 2010
The Copyright Acknowledgments on pages 209–210 constitute
an extension of this copyright page.

Manufactured in Canada.

LIBRARY AND ARCHIVES CANADA CATALOGUING IN PUBLICATION

The Penguin book of crime stories : volume II / selected and introduced
by Peter Robinson.

ISBN 978-0-14-317234-5

1. Crime—Fiction.   2. Detective and mystery stories, Canadian (English).
3. Detective and mystery stories, American.   4. Detective and mystery
stories, English.   5. Canadian fiction (English).   6. American fiction.
7. English fiction.   I. Robinson, Peter, 1950-   II. Title.

PN6120.95.D45P463 2010   C813'.087208   C2009-907529-6

Contents

Introduction

by

PETER ROBINSON

Short stories don't sell. Nobody reads short stories anymore. There are no markets for short stories. The short story is dead. These are statements one hears frequently in the world of short story writing. It is true that a slim volume of stories might represent a way into the rarefied atmosphere of the literary world for a young writer, but when it comes to stories that entertain or divert, that have plots, beginnings, middles, and ends—then the consensus is that most people prefer novels, thank you very much, and the thicker the better.

This applies most of all to that segregated and reviled branch of writing, genre fiction, where horror, crime, western, romance, and science fiction first blossomed in the late nineteenth or early twentieth century and formed the backbone of hundreds of magazines and newspapers. Demand was so high in the twenties and thirties that quality was bound to suffer, as some writers churned out story after story for the pulps to make a living. Now that there isn't anything like a living to be made from writing short stories, genre writers tend to approach the form as a challenge and as a way to spread their wings and move away, however briefly, from a successful series. Part of the appeal is also to work on something you can actually get the pleasure of finishing within a short period. While it is still true that a great deal of genre writing is dreadful, it is also true that a great deal of *all* writing is dreadful. But to paraphrase Longfellow's verse about the little girl with the curls, when crime writing is good, as it is here, it is very, very good.

Even though the markets have shrunk and many writers have turned away from the short story form, here we are with Volume II of *The Penguin Book of Crime Stories*, which contains stories as rich in skill and variety as any in the first collection. Within these pages, you will find the joy of rediscovering the old and familiar alongside the thrill of encountering a new voice for the first time. Almost all the writers included, such as Lee Child, Jeffery Deaver, Ruth Rendell, Reginald Hill, Sue Grafton, and John Connolly, are known primarily as crime novelists. Only Canada's James Powell has restricted himself to the short story, of which he has published over a hundred, starting in 1966, many in the pages of *Ellery Queen's Mystery Magazine*.

I do not feel I have to outline the history and development of the crime story back to Poe and Doyle again here, as I did in the first volume. There are more than enough sources for that information, and a reader could do much worse than picking up Julian Symons's excellent *Bloody Murder*. Any fan of crime fiction should read Symons's book, anyway.

Putting together an anthology of stories such as this is a joy from the editor's point of view. It is also full of surprises. Many well-known novelists have written few or no short stories, which sadly excludes a number of writers I would have liked to have included. I have tried, as in the previous volume, to get a representative selection from the United Kingdom, Canada, and the United States, and this time I have also included writers from the Republic of Ireland, South Africa, and Thailand. I would like to present an even more international selection—Scandinavia, for example, must be as rich in crime short stories as it is in novels—but finding stories in translation is often a problem. Perhaps this may be a project for the future. For now, though, despite their geographical variety, all the stories in this collection were written in English.

I made very few demands on the authors I approached, except that they submit a story they are particularly proud of and feel has been neglected. In that sense, the collection is the authors' choice. Most of the stories have been previously published, though often in anthologies that are now out of print and hard to find, but Sophie Hannah's "The Visitors' Book," for example, has only been broadcast on the UK's Radio 3, and though Colin Cotterill's "Forked" won an International Thriller Writers Association competition and appeared on an audiobook, it has never appeared in print.

Some authors found it difficult to make the final choice and submitted more than one tale. Joanna Kubicki, Dennis Richard Murphy's widow, for example, says, "I have selected two ... stories which I know he was quite proud of, and rightly so." I chose "Dead in the Water" because it is a particular favourite of mine. I know that Dennis would have been proud to see it reprinted in such august company. I also made selections from works submitted by Rick Mofina, Margie Orford, Robert J. Randisi, Sue Grafton, and Colin Cotterill, and it wasn't easy!

Some authors also gave reasons for choosing the story they did, and these can be revealing. Ruth Rendell, for example, says that she chose her story "Catamount" because "I loved the place it is set. It is in the heart of the Rocky Mountains of Colorado near the Yampa River valley. My son used to have a house there and it is one of the most beautiful places I have ever seen. There are lots of cougars, though I never saw one." Setting and a sense of place are often equally as important in a short story as in a novel, though the writer doesn't have quite so long to dwell on descriptive passages, and they can also act as an inspiration or a starting point. Place figures strongly in the stories by Dennis Richard Murphy, Sophie Hannah, and Margie Orford, among others. Of her story "The Meeting," Margie Orford says simply, "Here is a very Cape Town crime story ... atmospheric and not much police attention."

Just as a sense of place can be a trigger, so can a sense of history. James Powell, Maureen Jennings, and Barbara Fradkin all mine this vein with fascinating results. Forsaking her nineteenth-century Toronto sleuth, Murdoch, for Thomas More, Maureen Jennings says, "When I read the account of Sir Thomas More's head, I was tremendously moved and knew then I wanted to write a story about it. More's beloved daughter, Margaret Roper, was forced to beg for his severed head which was on a spike on Tower Bridge, with the heads of other men considered traitors to the mad Henry VIII. According to legend, an angel sent a wind to blow the head off and it fell into her boat. It's impossible to get more drama than that. I added a daub of fiction in the character of the bridge guard and wrote 'The Weeping Time.'"

James Powell finds an even more personal historical connection in "Clay Pillows" and demonstrates that memory and autobiographical detail can often have as powerful a presence in crime stories as they can elsewhere. Powell says, "I'm fond of this story in part because I was able to download some childhood memories into it: Toronto near the end of World War II; a trip to Niagara Falls with my mother in a borrowed car; visits back to the small southern Ontario town where my grandfather lived. Perhaps this is part of growing old, a getting things down on paper and safe from senior moments. In any event when I finished this story I found myself working on another about the memorable Toronto snowstorm of 1944–45 which shut my grade school down for three days."

Ottawa writer Barbara Fradkin, best known for her contemporary Inspector Green series, also takes a trip into the past with "Timber Town Justice," but it is, she maintains, "the ironic twist ending that makes it a favourite." You will find several ironic twists in these pages, as they have come to replace the whodunit plot twist in many modern crime stories. Instead of revealing the killer in a surprise ending, many writers choose to show us a different perspective on the tale they have just delivered, a reversal of viewpoint, and this is reflected in many of the stories included here.

You will find few traditional detective stories in this collection. Most series writers have forsaken their characters temporarily, though there is a fine Kinsey Millhone tale from Sue Grafton; Robert J. Randisi's Truxton Lewis appears in a case involving a St. Louis jazz club; Reginald Hill supplies a Dalziel and Pascoe yarn abounding with his customary wit and skill; and Margie Orford's criminal profiler Clare Hart makes an appearance in a frightening, claustrophobic story set in Cape Town's sprawling shantytown of Khayelitsha. Readers familiar with only the well-known series novels featuring John Connolly's Charlie Parker, Lee Child's Jack Reacher, Barbara Fradkin's Inspector Green, Colin Cotterill's septuagenarian coroner Dr. Siri Paiboun, Maureen Jennings's Murdoch, and Jeffery Deaver's Lincoln Rhyme, however, are in for a treat, as these writers take off in different directions. So dip in. A cornucopia of crime stories awaits you between these covers.

THE PENGUIN BOOK OF
CRIME STORIES
VOLUME II

The Game of Dog

by

REGINALD HILL

IT WAS CHARLEY FIELDS, the landlord of the Punchbowl, that started it. Like his great namesake, Charley didn't much care for dogs or children. In fact, being a Yorkshire publican down to his tap-roots, Charley didn't much care for anything except brass, Geoff Boycott, and his own way.

But if the price of getting the brass out of his customers' pockets into his till was admitting their little companions into his pub, he bit the bullet and said that as long as they didn't yap, fight, defecate or smell too high, they were welcome in the rather draughty and uncomfortable rear bar.

That was the children. The dogs were allowed in the cozy front snug under the same very reasonable conditions.

One misty October evening, Charley peered through the snug hatch to make sure no one was sitting there with an empty glass and he saw a scene to warm a canophilist's cockles.

In one corner, a terrier sat with its bright eyes fixed on the face of its owner who appeared to be dozing. Stretched out across the hearth in front of the glowing fire lay an aged bloodhound, looking as if it were carved out of bronze till the crinkling of cellophane brought its great head up to receive its tribute of barbecued beef flavour crisps. Beneath the window-nook table a border collie and a miniature poodle were sharing an ashtrayful of beer while above them their owners enjoyed one of those measured Yorkshire conversations that make Pinteresque dialogue sound like a Gilbert and Sullivan patter song. At the table by the door a small rough-haired mongrel, by dint of crawling round in ever decreasing circles, was contriving to bind the leg of its blissfully unaware owner to the leg of his chair.

This last was Detective Chief Inspector Peter Pascoe, the newest member of this canine club. The mongrel was Tig and belonged to his young daughter. As the nights drew in he didn't care to have her wandering the streets, even with such a fiercely defensive companion, so he'd taken over the evening walk whose turning point was the Punchbowl. Observing the bloodhound drooping in behind its owner one damp night, he'd followed suit and over the past couple of weeks he'd become almost a regular, though he never stayed long enough to exchange more than a polite good evening with the others nor to identify them beyond their dogs.

"Bugger me!" said Charley Field after drinking in the scene for a few moments. "You lot and your bloody dogs. You'd think you'd given birth to 'em! I bet if there were a fire and you'd only got time to rescue one human being or your dog, you lot wouldn't have to think twice!"

"Nay, Charley," said the poodle. "If it were thee, I'd not have to think once!"

Before Charley could respond to this sally he was summoned to the bar, leaving the poodle to enjoy the approving chuckles of his fellow drinkers.

As they died away the border collie suddenly said, "Hitler."

"Eh?"

"I'd rescue Floss here afore I'd rescue Hitler, no question."

The others considered. There was no dissent.

"Joe Stalin," said the poodle.

"The Yorkshire Ripper," said the bloodhound.

Both went through on the nod.

The collie looked towards the terrier, who still seemed to be dozing, then turned his gaze on Pascoe. He thought of explaining to them that as a policeman he was duty bound to regard all human life as sacred. Then he thought of trying to explain this to his daughter when he returned home with an incinerated Tig. Then he thought, lighten up, Pascoe. It's only pub talk!

"Maggie Thatcher?" he said tentatively.

This gave them pause.

"Nay," said the bloodhound. "She had her bad side, agreed, but she did some good things too. I don't think we can let her burn."

"I bloody could. Aye, and throw coals on the fire if I could find any to throw," growled the poodle. "She closed my pit and threw me and most of my mates on the slag heap, the cow."

The bloodhound looked ready to join issue, but the collie said, "Nay, we need to agree one hundred per cent on something like this."

And the terrier defused the situation entirely by suddenly sitting up straight, opening his eyes, and saying, "My mother-in-law!"

Over the next few weeks the game took shape, without formal rules but with rules that its participants instinctively understood, and their choice of candidates for the fire gave Pascoe more information about his fellow players than he was likely to get from general enquiry. In a Yorkshire pub a man's private life is a man's private life.

You can ask a direct question, but only if you can take an indirect answer. Pascoe on one occasion, finding himself alone with the bloodhound, had enquired casually what the man did for a living.

"I'm by way of being an expert," replied the bloodhound.

"Oh yes. An expert in what?"

"An expert in minding my own bloody business."

Which was reasonable enough, he decided, and had the upside of meaning he didn't have to tell them he was a policeman.

The one topic on which they all spoke freely was their dogs and Pascoe, by listening and by observation, was soon familiar with all their little ways. Fred, the ancient bloodhound, had three times been pronounced dead by the vet and three times given him the lie. He loved beef barbecue crisps and howled in derision if offered any other flavour. Floss, the collie, was a rescue dog, having been kicked off a farm when the farmer realized she was frightened of sheep. She was in love with Puff the poodle who shared her beer but showed no sign of wanting to share anything else, which was why his non-pc owner had changed his name from Percy. Tommy, the terrier, was a genius. He could die for England, stand on his hind legs and offer left or right paw as requested. His *pièce de résistance,* when given the command *Light!,* was to go to the fireplace, extract one of the wooden spills from a container standing on the grate, insert it in the flame and bring it back to light its master's cigarette. Tig always watched this performance with a sort of sneering yawn. The human race, apart from Rosie Pascoe whom he adored, was there to serve dogs, not the other way round. He didn't want any dog's nose up his behind that had already been up a human's.

The one thing the dogs had in common was that their owners could all find someone, indeed several someones, whom they asserted they would put beneath their pets on a rescue priority list, and the Game soon became a regular part of their evening encounter, its rules established by intuitive agreement rather than formal debate.

It was always initiated by someone saying, "Hitler!" Thereafter the others spoke as the spirit moved them. Approval of a nomination was signified by an aye or a nod, and if unanimous, the game moved on. In the event of objection, the proposer was given a fair hearing after which objectors either stated their case or admitted themselves persuaded. Unless the vote was unanimous, the nominee was declared saved. And the game was usually closed by the terrier declaring, "My mother-in-law!" though it was possible for someone else to close it by calling out, "*His* mother-in-law!"

Pascoe, after his initial failure with Mrs. Thatcher, restricted himself to historical characters. Nero was given a universal thumbs-down and he successfully argued the case for leaving Richard the Third to the flames, but when he ventured closer to living memory and suggested Field Marshall Haig who commanded the British Forces in the First World War, he met surprising opposition and failed to carry the field. On the other hand, it was only his unyielding opposition which pulled the fingers of the Hand of God, Diego Maradona, out of the fire.

When he explained the game to his wife, Ellie, she wrinkled her nose in distaste and said, *"Men!"* "Hang about," he protested. "It's only a bit of fun. Anyway, you tell me, you've got the choice between saving Tig and saving George Bush, who do you grab?" "That's what I mean," she said. "This stuff's too serious to make a game out of." To which he replied, *"Women!"*

One December evening when the frost was so sharp that even Tig's normal indifference to sub-zero temperatures was sorely tested, the pair of them burst into the snug like a pair of Arctic explorers discovering a Little Chef at the Pole.

They got as close as they could to the roaring fire without standing on the bloodhound and gave themselves over to the delicious agony of defrosting. It wasn't till the process was sufficiently advanced to make him admit the wisdom of stepping back a foot or so that Pascoe became aware that the atmosphere in the room, though physically warm, was distinctly depressed. His greeting had been answered by a series of noncommittal grunts and even the dogs looked subdued.

He went to the hatch and attracted Charley Field's attention.

"I'll have a scotch tonight, Charley," he said. Then, lowering his voice, he asked, "What's up with this lot? I've seen livelier wakes."

"You're not so far wrong," said Charley. "You've not heard about Lenny then?"

So used was he to thinking about the others only in terms of their dogs, it took Pascoe a moment to work out that Lenny was Tommy the terrier's owner who was absent tonight.

"No. What?"

"There was a fire at his house last night."

"Oh God. Is he all right?'

"He's fine."

"And Tommy?"

"He's fine too."

Pascoe thought for a second and didn't like where his thoughts were taking him.

"Was anyone hurt?" he asked.

"Aye," said Charley Field. "His mother-in-law. Burnt to a cinder."

THE FOLLOWING MORNING Detective Superintendent Andy Dalziel sat listening to Peter Pascoe with growing disbelief.

When he'd finished the Fat Man said, "I had a dream the other night. Wieldy came to see me to say he were getting married to Prince Charles and it was going to be a white wedding and he wanted my advice on whether he should sell the photo rights to *Hello!* or *OK.*"

"And which did you go for?"

"I went downstairs for a stiff drink. But thinking about it, I reckon my dream made more sense than what you've just told me."

He looked at the local paper spread out on his desk. Its headline was THE HERO OF HARTSOP AVENUE over a photo of a man with a terrier in his arms and a blanket round his shoulders being comforted by a fireman outside a smouldering house. The legend below read *Mr. Leonard Gold (38) returned from a meeting at the Liberal Club to find his house in Hartsop Avenue ablaze. Knowing that his mother-in-law, Mrs. Brunnhilde Smith (62), was still in the building, despite all efforts to stop him, he rushed inside in an attempt to rescue her. Unhappily his courageous act was in vain; the fire was too far advanced for him to reach the upstairs room from which Mrs. Smith's body was later recovered, and it was only the arrival of the fire brigade that enabled Mr. Gold himself to make his escape.*

"Let me get this straight," said Dalziel. "This guy's a hero, nearly gets burned to death trying to rescue his ma-in-law, ends up in hospital being treated for second degree burns, and because of some daft game some dog fanciers play in a pub, you want to investigate him for choosing to get his dog out and leaving the old girl to fry? Have I got the gist?"

"That's about it," said Pascoe.

"And have you got any evidence to support this, apart from this dog game you play?"

"No," said Pascoe. "But I haven't looked into it yet. I only heard about the fire last night and I wanted to run it past you first."

"I think you need to run a lot bloody faster," said Dalziel. "Preferably out of my sight. Have you got nowt better to do, like for instance your job? Best keep your hobbies for your own time."

"In actual fact," said Pascoe prissily, "this is my own time. I've got the day off, remember? But in any case, I always thought the investigation of suspicious death was a large part of my job."

"Suspicious? Has anyone from the Fire Department been in touch with us to say there's something dodgy about the fire? Or anyone from the path lab to say they've got worries about the way the old girl died?"

"No. But it's not that kind of suspicion."

"So what kind of suspicion is it, Pete? I mean, even supposing what you say is true, where's the sodding crime?"

"I'm sure there's got to be something," said Pascoe. "I'll ring up the CPS and talk to a lawyer, shall I?"

"If you must," sighed Dalziel. "And while you're at it ask 'em which they'd go for, *Hello!* or *OK.*"

IT WASN'T OFTEN that the CPS and Andy Dalziel were in accord, but this seemed to be one of those occasions.

The lawyer he spoke to was a young woman called appropriately Portia Silk, who had what might have been in other circumstances an infectious laugh, which he heard as she quoted at him, "Thou shalt not kill but need'st not strive Officiously to keep alive."

"But surely if you let someone die when you could have saved them ..." he protested, whereupon she interrupted with, "Only if you have a professional relationship as in doctor/patient, or a duty of care as in teacher/pupil. But if you're walking along the canal bank and you see someone struggling in the water, it may be regarded by some people as reprehensible of you not to dive in and try to save them, but it's not a criminal act. Even if it were, in the circumstances you cite, proving deliberate choice of dog over woman would be very difficult."

Pascoe had not survived and prospered under the despotic rule of Andy Dalziel by being easily deterred from a chosen path, and after his disappointing talk with Ms. Silk, he immediately dialled the Fire Station and had a chat with Keith Little, the Fire Officer who'd been given the job of looking at the Hartsop Avenue blaze.

"No, nothing suspicious else we'd have been on to you. Fire started downstairs in the living room. Dead woman was a chain smoker by all accounts. From the look of things, fire started in an old sofa in the sitting room, fag end down between the cushions which predated the fire retardant regulations, and eventually you'd get nice little fire going which once it burnt through to the stuffing would really explode. After that, well it's an old house, wooden floors, wooden beams, even wood panelling on some of the walls. Some of them old places are bonfires just waiting for someone to toss a match on to them. Why are you asking, by the way? You got a sniff of something iffy?"

"No," replied Pascoe honestly. "Just curiosity. It was in my neck of the woods and I know Mr. Gold slightly. You've spoken to him?"

"Yeah. He's still in hospital. Hero, they're calling him. Right idiot in my book. Two of our lads had to go in there to get him out. Found him crouched down in the shower room, half unconscious from smoke inhalation. Could have cost them their lives too if things had gone wrong."

"Did they get the dog out as well? The one he's holding in the *Evening News* picture."

"No. I gather it were waiting for him when our boys brought him out. They remarked what a fuss it made of him. The paramedics had to let it in the ambulance with him. If you want to be loved, get a dog, eh?"

"Wasn't there a window in the shower room?"

"Aye, but far too small for a grown man."

"Where did they find the dead woman?"

"Her room was right above the sitting room. Seems her favourite hobby is lying on her bed with a bottle of vodka and listening to music full blast. She'd not have heard anything. In fact it's likely if she'd drunk enough, she'd have died in her sleep afore the fire erupted through the floorboards. Let's hope so. No way our lads could get to her. They did well to get our sodding hero out."

When a further call to the pathology lab confirmed that Mrs. Smith had indeed been asphyxiated by smoke inhalation before the flames got to work on her, it seemed to Pascoe he'd reached the end of the road. Ellie hadn't been all that pleased when he'd announced that morning that despite having the day off, there was something he had to check out at work, so now he made his exit before the Fat Man found him something to do.

Hartsop Avenue was a mile and half the far side of the Punchbowl from where Pascoe lived and there was no reason for him to go anywhere near it on his way home. Nevertheless, somehow or other he found himself parked outside the burnt-out shell of the Gold house thirty minutes later.

He got out of his car and stood looking at the wrecked building. Two women walked by him, carrying shopping bags. As they passed, one said to the other in a deliberately loud voice, "I think it's disgusting the way some people make an entertainment out of other folks' disasters."

She then turned into the gateway of the house next door while her companion went on her way.

Pascoe hurried towards the neighbour, pulling his warrant card out of his pocket.

"Excuse me," he called.

She turned an unfriendly face towards him, but when she saw the card, her manner became conciliatory.

"I'm sorry what I said just now," she apologized. "I thought you were just one of them sightseers. We had a lot of them yesterday, just walking or driving by to take a look. Ghouls, I call them."

"I agree," said Pascoe. "But it's human nature, I'm afraid. You know the Golds well, do you?"

"Oh yes. Greta, that's Mrs. Gold, is staying with us till they get something sorted out. Poor woman, she's devastated."

"I gather she was away when it happened."

"Down in London, visiting an old school friend and doing some Christmas shopping. *She* wanted to go too, but I think Greta's friend made it quite clear the invitation was for Greta only."

She Pascoe took to refer to Brunnhilde Smith.

"So you got on well with the Golds then?"

"Oh yes. Lovely couple. Very quiet. At least they were till *she* came to live with them. But I shan't speak ill of the dead."

Pascoe's long experience recognized this as the precursor of ill-speaking in the same way as a wassailer in a Danish mead-hall knew that *Hwaet!* signalled the start of *Beowulf.*

Two minutes later he was seated in Mrs. Woolley's kitchen drinking tea and listening to an account of Lennie Gold's mother-in-law which put her on a par with Grendel's mother.

Mrs. Woolley was a friend and confidante of Greta Gold and had got the family background from her. It seemed her mother, Brunnhilde Hotter, a native of Hanover, had married a British soldier in the sixties and on his demob, they'd settled in London where Greta was born. She'd married Lennie Gold in 1985, and they made the error of setting up home only ten minutes drive from Greta's family home in Kilburn. By 1990, Lennie had had enough. Despite being a Londoner born and bred, he started looking for a job as far away from the capital as he could get, which in the event turned out to be Mid-Yorkshire.

"Everything was fine," said Mrs. Woolley. "She came visiting occasionally, but you can put up with a short visit, can't you? So long as you can see an end. And Mr. Smith never liked to be away from home too long. Then five years ago he died. Naturally Greta made her mother come and stay with her for a while to help her come to terms with things. Couple of weeks, she thought. Month at the most. Well, the way Greta put it, there was never a time when they actually asked her to live with them permanently, but somehow it just happened. Hilda— that's what she got—Brunnhilde's too much of a mouthful—Hilda had a bad leg. Circulatory problem she said. Fat problem I said. Human limbs weren't made for that kind of load bearing. She was a big woman, must have cost a fortune to feed. I've seen her sitting where you are now, Mr. Pascoe, and watched her eat the whole of one of my Victoria sponges, four slices and it was gone. Plus I had to get my husband to strengthen the chair she sat on, she left it so wobbly."

As well as her dietary excesses, there were plenty of other strikes against the Widow Smith, according to Mrs. Woolley. She was a chain smoker, she dominated conversations, she often said things in German to her daughter which were clearly comments on others present too rude to be spoken in English, she liked to lie on her bed and play her favourite records very loud ("Wagner, it was," said Mrs. Woolley. "I know because George, that's my husband, he likes that kind of stuff, but he listens through his headphones, knowing I can't put up with all that screeching and howling"), she complained bitterly to any who couldn't avoid listening that it was a tragedy her Greta had married such a useless idle man as Lennie ("One time she said to me," said Mrs. Woolley, "she said, *don't you think that's a Jew name, Lennie Gold? All right, they got married in a church but I have seen him coming out of the shower and his thing was like a skinned rabbit.* I told her live and let live, she should be ashamed saying such things but she just laughed and tapped her nose"). And above or beneath all she hated Tommy, saying the dog was unhygienic, and she was allergic, and it ought to be put down. ("Such a nice little dog," concluded Mrs. Woolley. "And so clever. I bet if it was one of those things like wolves they had at Colditz, she'd have been a bit fonder of it!")

With the woman's permission Pascoe wandered out into the garden and looked up at the burnt-out shell next door. The garage was on this side, its sloping roof joining the main house wall just below a small square window which was closed, though its glass was cracked, presumably by the heat of the fire.

"Right mess, isn't it?" said a cheerful voice.

He turned to see a round bald man who introduced himself as George Woolley.

"That window," said Pascoe. "Is that the shower room where they found Lennie?"

Woolley confirmed that it was.

"Like a door it was to that dog," he went on. "Lenny used to leave it open for Tommy so he could get out to do his business when he was shut in the house by himself. A bloody marvel, that dog. Many's the time I've seen him hop out, run down the garage roof, jump down onto the rain barrel there, do the job, then head back in the same way."

"But the window's closed," said Pascoe. "Presumably Lennie didn't bother to open it last night because he wasn't leaving Tommy shut in the house by himself. Mrs. Smith was there."

"*Her*" said Woolley with the same intonation as his wife. "She'd not have bothered to let him out even if she'd noticed he wanted to go. In fact she'd rather he messed up in the house so that she'd have something else to complain about."

"You don't seem to have liked her much," said Pascoe.

"Sorry, I know she's dead, but I'm not going to lie. She was a pain and I doubt if even Greta will mind very much that she's gone, not once she gets over the first shock. No, if Lenny had been killed trying to save her, that would have been the real tragedy. I couldn't believe it when he set off into the house ..."

"You were there?" said Pascoe.

"Oh yes. I'd been at the Liberal Club with him. Not that we're Liberals. Who is, these days? But it's a good pint and not too pricey."

"But he didn't take Tommy?"

"No. No dogs in the club, that's the rule." He grinned and added, "And no women either, except on Ladies' Night. Oh yes, it's a grand place."

"It sounds it. So where did he leave Tommy? He can't have been in the house, can he?"

"I suppose not. He's got a kennel in the garden, and sometimes he stays out there when the weather's fine."

"I see. And you came back together from the club …" prompted Pascoe.

"That's right. In my car. We turned into the Avenue and I said hello! What's going off? We could see one or two people standing around and it's usually dead quiet. Then Lenny said, oh my God, it's my house! Well the ground floor was already well alight. I knew that Hilda must still be in there; there was a light on in her bedroom and you could hear her hi-fi system belting out Wagner. Lenny jumped out of the car, I've never seen him so agitated. He didn't seem to know what to do with himself. I asked someone if they'd rung the brigade and they said yes. Lenny ran up the side of the house, I presume to see if he could get in the back, then he appeared at the front again. I got hold of him and said, it's no use, Lenny, we can't do anything, the fire brigade will be here any minute. But he broke loose and before I could do anything he was up the path and going in the front door. I went after him, but the heat was too much for me. I could hear the sirens in the distance and knew that help wouldn't be long, but I really did fear the worst. And what made it worse was Tommy came running round the side of the house, barking and agitated, like he knew Lenny was in there. I've never been so relieved in my life as I was when the firemen brought him out, and I thought Tommy was going to have a fit, he was so happy. He's at the hospital too, you know. Against all the rules, but there was no separating the two of them."

"Yes, they really worship each other, don't they?"

"That's right. Hey, does that mean you know Lenny and Tommy?"

"Yes. In fact I meet them sometimes when I'm out with my dog."

"That explains it," said Woolley, smiling. "I was wondering what a cop was doing looking around after the fire. So it's just personal interest, is it?"

"Oh yes. I live quite close and I thought, knowing Lenny, that I'd take a look," said Pascoe, feeling rather guilty as he uttered the lie.

"Understandable," said Woolley. "You're not thinking of visiting him in hospital by any chance, are you?"

"I suppose I might, some time," said Pascoe vaguely.

"It's just that I'd told my wife I'd take her in at lunchtime and we'd bring Greta home and make sure she got a bite of lunch. That's why I'm back here now, but to tell the truth it hasn't gone down too well at work, there's a meeting I should be at in half an hour's time, and there's no way I'd be able to make it ... but if you were going to the hospital to see Lennie ..."

Why not? thought Pascoe. His morning was knackered anyway, and his suspicions, which had been looking more and more stupid over the past half hour, had left him feeling very guilty.

He said, "Yes, I could do that."

"Great! You're a star! I'll just tell my good lady."

As they went back into the house, Woolley suddenly laughed and said, "I know I shouldn't but I had to smile when I thought about it later ..."

"What?"

"Do you know your Wagner, Mr. Pascoe?"

"A bit."

"Well, when we got out of the car and saw the house burning, the music blasting out of the upstairs window was *Gotterdammerung*. It was that bit right at the end when they've lit Siegfried's funeral pyre. Brunnhilde gets on her horse and sends him plunging into the heart of the flames. Ironic, eh?"

"Always good for a laugh, old Wagner," said Peter Pascoe.

AT THE HOSPITAL, they found Lenny Gold fast asleep in a small private room. His wife was with him, and so was Tommy, who greeted Pascoe like an old friend.

Greta Gold, a slender, pale-faced woman with more of the Rhine maiden about her than the Valkyrie, said, "They let me bring him, but I have to take him away with me. He doesn't mind. I think he understands he can come back."

"I'm sure he does," said Pascoe. "He's a very clever dog. I know how fond Lenny is of him."

"Yes, he is," said Greta, smiling at the terrier. "Sometimes I'd tell him I thought he loved the dog more than me."

"Nonsense," said Mrs. Woolley. "Lenny adores you."

"I know he does. I was only joking. But Tommy means such a lot to him. Sometimes if we were out for a long time, he would even ring home, just so Tommy could hear his voice on the answer machine and be reassured. I'm so glad we didn't lose him too, that would have been too much to bear …"

Her eyes filled with tears. Mrs. Woolley put her arm round her shoulder and led her aside.

Pascoe stood awkwardly by the bed, looking down at the sleeping figure. His hands were encased in plastic bags to protect the dressings and his face and head had been scorched too. All this suffered in his brave attempt to save a woman he had every cause to hate, thought Pascoe, his guilt returning with advantages.

Mrs. Woolley said, "I'm just taking Greta down to the waiting room for a cup of tea, Mr. Pascoe. We won't be long."

"Yes. That will be fine."

The two women left. Tommy showed signs of wanting to accompany them, but Pascoe called, "Tommy, come. Down. Stay."

The dog trotted back, lay down under the bed, and looked up at him, its eyes bright, its ears pricked waiting for the next command.

Pascoe thought of Tig's likely reaction to such an instruction. He might obey in the end, but it would involve a lot of thought and a great deal of yawning. Much as he loved the little mongrel, it must be nice to have a pet who didn't regard you as inferior, to whom your every word was like the voice of God …

God which is dog backward … the Game of Dog … the Game of God …

Into his mind came an image of Tommy lying in his basket in front of the fire in the Golds' parlour. The phone rings. After a while the answer machine switches on. The voice of God says, "Tommy." His ears prick. He sits up. The voice of God says, "Light!" He goes to the fireplace, picks up a spill of wood left there, sticks it through the bars of the guard, and when it catches, he takes it to … where? To, say, the sofa, where a cigarette has been left stuck between two cushions. He lights the cigarette, drops the spill, gets back into his basket. And the cigarette burns, and the spill burns, and the cushion … perhaps a small section of the cushion had had something rubbed into it, one of those cleaning solutions, for instance, which the instructions warn are highly inflammable …

The fire starts. The dog becomes aware of it. After a while he realizes this is something it would be a good idea to distance himself from. He wanders up the stairs to his usual exit, the shower room window.

But it is closed.

Brunnhilde, either because she thinks there's a draught, or out of sheer malice and in the hope that Lenny will be confronted by a dog mess on his return, has closed it. As the smoke drifts up the stairs, Tommy starts barking. But his warning cries are drowned by *The Twilight of the Gods* at full belt, and Brunnhilde on her bed is too deep into her vodka bottle and too immersed in Wagner's Germanic flames to be aware of this puny Anglo-Saxon fire building up beneath her.

Lenny comes home. He expects to be greeted by Tommy. When the dog doesn't appear, he rushes down the side of the house and sees that the shower room window has been closed.

And now in panic he returns to the front. The fire roars, the heat is intense. But Tommy is in there. He breaks free from his friend's grasp and rushes into the flames. He knows where Tommy will be. He opens the window, urges the dog out.

And then because he fears, probably foolishly, that the dog's love may match his own, he pulls the window shut again in case Tommy tries to get back in to be by his side. And he sinks to the floor and prepares to die.

A story of great ingenuity ...

A story of great villainy ...

A story of great courage ...

A story of such absurdity that Pascoe shuddered at the thought of Andy Dalziel even suspecting that his right hand man had let it pollute his mind.

Such ludicrous fantasies belonged, if anywhere, to the world of fairy tales, of escapist movies, of childish parlour games.

Like the Game of Dog.

He mouthed a silent *sorry* at the poor burnt hero who lay before him.

Lenny's eyes opened.

He looked up, focused, and recognition dawned.

He tried to say something.

Tommy, aware his master was conscious, put his front paws on the bed and raised his head to the level of the pillow, his tail wagging furiously.

Lenny reached out one of his bagged hands, touched the terrier's head and winced.

Then he looked at Pascoe and smiled and winked, and tried to speak again.

"What?" said Pascoe, stooping closer.

"Hitler!" said Lennie.

Forked

by

COLIN COTTERILL

THE PIANO TUNER closed his eyes and listened to the notes as they climbed to the arched ceiling of the recital hall. Passersby in Warsaw's Old Market Square paused to enjoy the ascending chords and riffs played by a man confident in his relationship with the heavy ivory keys. These were the last notes he would ever play and there was no lasting memory of them save a distant hum in his mind. He closed the lid and wiped away his tears with a large white handkerchief. The piano was pitch perfect. Only he was out of tune now.

On the flight home he used the headphones as a barrier between him and the gum augmentation specialist beside him. He refused refreshments, closed his eyes and considered what he could expect at Heathrow. He decided it would be informal: conservatively British. Not, he imagined, a wail of sirens or a flash of black flak jackets passing in front of his eyes like a bump on the head. Rather, a nod from the turbaned immigration officer and the approach of a tall young man with a neck bearing wounds from a cheap razor. Beside him a dark-skinned female in a black suit—the younger sister of a Jamaican undertaker, perhaps. A slight self-consciously polite nod from the young man and the words,

"Thomas Cedric Cooksley?"

Thomas would not render them unconscious with a series of strategically placed blows and sprint back into the labyrinth of tunnels. He would not commandeer a baggage tractor and flee across a busy runway. The police were there at his invitation so he would nod and smile politely, perhaps ask them if they were well.

"You are under arrest for the murder of Mrs. Evangaline Victoria Cooksley."

This would be followed by a brief caution, an unobtrusive hand around the arm, and an escorted stroll to a waiting police car. In England, such matters were dealt with in a far more civilized fashion than across the Atlantic.

Not wanting to leave matters in the hands of an incompetent investigator, when he'd phoned the Metropolitan Police emergency line three days earlier and made his confession, he had provided them with the date and time of his arrival from Europe. He hadn't given them the flight number because he preferred to be arrested nicely on his home soil, not bundled into a Polish police car, beaten senseless and manhandled home by two neckless goons. He requested just one last period of dignity before joining the ranks of the criminal class.

In case they thought his call was a hoax he'd given them his home address, 32 Ridley Road, Hammersmith, West London, and told them it wouldn't be necessary to break down the door because there was a key under the front door mat. He knew the police would be dismayed at the thought but he explained that it was sewn into a small pocket on the underside of the mat. The only danger was that somebody might steal the mat itself. He explained that they would find his wife on the floor of their bedroom in front of his mother-in-law's oak dressing table. She could be identified by the pale blue house coat with small dark blue Chinese dragons on the lapels and a tuning fork embedded in her left eye. The fork was premium nickel-plated with an uncustomarily long handle.

He'd given that fork a good deal of thought over the past three days and nights. He'd wondered, given its peculiar shape, exactly how he'd been able to kill her with it. Firstly, it must have taken tremendous force to be able to pierce her eye. How was a man as meek as he able to summon such power? That was a question he imagined his solicitor might ask the court at his trial. But there had to be no more doubt of his abilities. The only way he might avoid this question would be to do without a lawyer and represent himself. He could then choose not to ask himself such questions. But the British legal system strongly discouraged self-representation, so he'd need a strong rebuttal. It would be this: that forty years of living with a woman who constantly reminded him of his one major failing can well up in a man however timid. He'd been driven to distraction by hearing again and again how badly she'd married. She'd believed her fiancé would become a well-known concert pianist, but look what she'd ended up with, a piano tuner.

"You had the acumen," she would remind him. "You had the technical ability. It's unthinkable that you were unable to make a name for yourself on the international circuit. Pathetic!"

Of course it was thinkable because it had happened. A number of young men and women every bit as talented as he had graduated from the Royal Academy. Yes, for acumen and technical skills he was in the top five percent. But modern music had sought to compete for fans with the other musical genres. It wasn't pianos people came to look at, it was the impresarios who tamed the beasts: the personalities, the eccentricities, the sex. The piano was no longer an instrument, it was a dance partner, a lover. If a pianist could do no more than sit for three hours, dead from the wrists upward, modern audiences would elect to stay home and spend their money on a decent music system. Sadly, Thomas Cooksley had no personality of which the piano might become an extension. His music was vibrant but he himself was dull. His piano had multiple orgasms while he snoozed at the keyboard.

And, over those forty years, barely a day went by when she didn't remind him in one way or another.

"Cornflakes? We could be eating fresh muesli on a balcony over-looking Lake d'Orta if you'd just fulfilled your potential."

Yes, that was where the force came from. That, to the utter surprise of the Crown prosecution, is what he'd own up to—no inadequacies in Thomas Cooksley.

"The hate built over forty years till one day it exploded in me."

But, surprised as he was that he had the strength to bury a tuning fork into his wife's eye, he was even more surprised that it could kill her. He was looking forward to hearing the coroner's report at the trial. There had been remarkably little blood. He had two theories of his own. His first was that the fork had punctured her brain. The C pitch had reverberated through her cranium and tuned her senseless. The second, and more likely scenario, was that she had turned to the mirror, seen a tuning fork protruding from her eye, and had a heart attack. Her heart was no stronger than her fidelity. Either way she was just as dead.

If he were to be honest, he'd been more concerned about the cat than his wife. He'd arrived at Heathrow to catch his flight, called the Metropolitan Police to confess, and was sitting in the departure lounge reading the *Daily Express* when he remembered Ginger. Their cat of many years was almost entirely confined to the house and a small patch of garden around the back door. His fence-climbing days were far behind him. Thomas doubted the police would open a can of Whiskas chopped liver and wait around long enough for him to relieve himself of it. But Ginger was a good-mannered beast and he would have allowed himself to blow up rather than defecate in the house.

So, Thomas had called the senior partner of his two-man piano tuning company, Alistair McWiggen, the grand old queen of Queen Anne Grands.

"Wiggy," he'd said. "It's me."

"Ye Gods. You've missed your flight. Heaven help us. The Warsaw Symphony and we've let them down." He made a fainting sound with his breath.

It was unthinkable that Thomas might miss an appointment or let down the firm.

"Don't get into a flap old girl. I'm at the airport. It's just there's been a little to-do at my house."

To the accompaniment of squeals and shrieks, he'd explained his predicament. By the time he got around to asking the big soft fairy if he'd be so kind as to look after his cat, the senior partner was aflood with tears. It was uncertain whether the message had been received, but by then they had announced Thomas's flight for the third time. Warsaw beckoned. Ginger was entrusted to fate.

THE AIRPLANE'S MEANDERING TAXI JOURNEY around the Heathrow tarmac took almost as long as the flight itself. When finally they found a vacant gate, Thomas was surprised at how unwobbly his legs were, how confident his stride. He joined the passport queue and scanned the far side of the booths for the tall white and short black. He handed his passport to the unsmiling Sikh and was surprised that the picture therein still bore a passing resemblance to the murderer at the front of the immigration line.

"Welcome home, Mr. Cooksley," the bearded man said and handed back the passport. It wasn't a greeting; merely one of a list of "phrases to make our officers seem like they care," plucked from the manual. To Thomas it sounded like a bluff. Until he was moved along by security, he stood awaiting his arrest in the area clearly marked "No Waiting." He allowed his mind to trip over possibilities. Perhaps the Met hadn't believed him—hadn't bothered to visit his house. Perhaps they had the wrong date, or had become tired of waiting. Perhaps, heaven forbid, Eva wasn't dead. She'd answered the doorbell with a towel over her head pretending to be fresh from the shower. No, no, she'd had no pulse. She hadn't so much as flinched when he kicked her. He was certain she'd be smelling to high heaven by now. What if the cat had eaten parts of her then exploded all over the new bedroom wallpaper? The possibilities were too awful to consider.

The uncertainty, the unexpected, these were what set off a tremor in Thomas's old legs and a flutter in his stomach. He could tolerate the suspense for no longer than was absolutely necessary. He ignored the Underground sign and went straight to the taxi stand out front. The rates were exorbitant and there probably wouldn't be much change from the Warsaw cheque, but he had to get home as soon as possible. The East African driver was in no more of a mood for conversation than his passenger. He noted the address and dedicated himself to his task. It was the type of February day when the dirty clouds squatted low over the streets and suffocated the buildings. It was like driving through a carwash in a grey cave. The driver swore in Kiswahili every time a truck kicked up filthy water onto his windows.

Thomas imagined a dark novel in which the protagonist was off to confront a situation worse than death. No writer could have painted a more dour journey than West London at four-thirty on a drizzly Wednesday. Every dripping person they passed had a shadow of doom tattooed on his face. Each oncoming headlight flashed a warning of the dread it was escaping. After an hour they came off the A4 and began to angle through the gloomy suburbs whose lights seemed low on batteries—a country that dispensed daylight so sparingly could surely invest in streetlights that offered more than a duckpond of light every twenty yards.

Thirty-two Ridley Road feigned innocence from the outside. It stood solid and bleak, unable to breathe through the rain that beat against its facade. Its glass was black. Its brick was pitted with neglect. As the taxi pulled away, Thomas stood on the pavement letting the cold rain soak into his woollen suit—his raincoat over his arm. His wheeled case stood beside him like a black retriever awaiting its master's signal to go forward.

The key was in its pocket under the doormat and when he turned the metal in the lock it sounded to him like a dentist removing a tooth with pliers. He let the door swing open but remained on the step. He looked into the darkness and, without question, the darkness looked back at him. He flicked on the passage light and took in a deep breath. All he could smell was *pot pourri*. According to the television, the stench of a body three days into its decay should be vile enough to peel paint. Either Evangeline's body was no longer in the house, or Evangeline was not dead.

With the front door wide open behind him, the uninvited rain rudely blowing through it, he walked to the staircase and turned the dimmer switch for the upstairs landing. From the bottom step he could see the top of the master bedroom door. Something was odd downstairs but his mind was racing, already on the landing. As he climbed the creaky staircase, more and more of the bedroom came into view until he was standing in front of it. He sniffed again.

Nothing. The bedroom light switch was a yard inside the door and in order to reach it he had to take a step into the shadow. He was fumbling across the wallpaper when he heard the voice from the bed.

"Hello, Thomas. I've been waiting for you."

Thomas stumbled back against the frame of the door. His legs gave up on him completely and he slid down onto the blue shag carpeting. He could barely make out a shadow on the high mattress. It reached for the bedside lamp and clicked the button. The piano tuner's mouth fell open with the weight of a hangman's trap door. His damp eyes took in the pale blue housecoat with its dragon lapels, the incongruous fluffy pink slippers, and the long brown hair. Had it occurred to Thomas to breathe at all during his journey to the upper floor, he might not have passed out. As he'd never fainted before, and believed it to be a condition reserved exclusively for frail and easily shocked women, he assumed he was dying.

IT WAS IMPOSSIBLE TO TELL how long Thomas had been unconscious. His partner, Alistair, stood to one side of the bed wringing a flannel into a small plastic bowl. As always, he was impeccably dressed in a tweed waistcoat and bow tie. He opened up the cloth and placed it above Thomas's eyebrows. As his forehead extended all the way to the back there had been no need to fold it. It felt painfully ice cold and sent a shudder down the junior partner's spine.

"Did you see her?" Thomas asked.

"Oh, I certainly did, my sweets."

"I thought she was dead. I was certain …"

"And you were totally spot on to believe so, Thomas."

"But …?"

"Look, I'm such a Wally-wanker, I admit it. I'd been waiting for you to get back. Couldn't resist trying on some of Eva's things one last time. I dropped off. Can you find it in your heart to forgive me?"

Thomas sat up.

"Why haven't I been arrested? Didn't the police come to find Anj?"

"They did, darling. They did."

"And?"

"And they met her."

"Wiggy, you're giving me a worse headache than I deserve."

"You called me from the airport. You told me you'd confessed to the police."

"Yes?"

"And I got here before them. Justice moves slowly in Grande Bretagne. I almost gave myself a hernia putting her body in your old W. H. Paling Upright downstairs."

"You put her in the piano? But you said they'd met her."

"Well, technically. You see, Evangeline and I are the same size. And she does have … or, I suppose I have to say, did have a splendid range of rather expensive cosmetics."

"You passed yourself off as Anj? Wiggy, how could you?"

"Why not? Anj didn't look like Anj without her face on. I was more than a passing resemblance to your dead wife."

"They believed you were a woman?"

"Absolutely, darling."

"McWiggen?"

"All right, perhaps not entirely sucked in. But they did believe we had 'a relationship' at some level. The modern bobby is rather more broadminded than we give him credit for. They asked to have a look around. They saw all our holiday snaps and our bedroom, minus one soiled Afghan rug. I told them about our little fight and how you like to get your bitchy revenge on me. I cried a little and talked them out of pressing charges against you for filing a falsie. And they left. Rather dashing young sergeant. I almost cracked a feel as he was leaving but that would have been pushing the dildo a touch, don't you think?"

"Where's Anj?"

"I nailed down the lid of your piano and had Alan and Bertrand come by to pick it up and take it to the workshop. That night I gave myself another hernia hauling the slovenly bitch out and into the truck. I took her for a ride to the new concert hall they're building at Burgh Heath. The cement in one of the pillar foundations was just damp enough. I could probably have found somewhere closer to bury her but, given her desire to be on the concert circuit, I thought it was charmingly fitting. Don't you?"

"Wiggy, I thought you liked her."

"Loathed her, sweetheart. Loathed her. I detested the way she put you down all the time. But she was your wife and it wasn't my place. I've been saying a little prayer beside my bed all these years that you'd take an axe to her."

"You did all this for me?"

"Isn't it brilliant, the things a man would do for love?"

Dead in the Water

by

DENNIS RICHARD MURPHY

IT WAS ME killed The Painter.

I missed his first trip to The Park. While Matty Mattoonen and Laurence Dalton were guiding him out of Mowat, I was paddling Miss Katie Mattoonen toward the creek that runs from Canoe into Bonita Lake. Laurence Dalton got me a couple of beers without telling Matty who was pretty nervous about his two girls and was always on about how he wanted "the best for them." I didn't think Jaako Koskinen qualified as the best of anything, but he'd married the older sister Doris.

Back in 1900, upwards of 700 people lived in Mowat around Gilmour's sawmill. The spur line ran up a mile to the north end of Potter's Creek and Canoe Lake Station. We'd skip school on those warm days when the thaw had set in and hitch rides on the lumber cars hauled up to join the main train. We'd hang around the Station until old Mrs. Ratan shooed us out, then we'd walk back to town, trying to balance on the hot steel rails, tossing rocks into the creek and arguing about whether the pile in the path was scat from a marten or shit from a wolverine.

The Park was where I was from, more than a dirty old logging town like Mowat. The Park and me was both born in 1893, so I grew up feeling like it was my brother. My parents were dead from a bush accident so The Park was family, and even a teacher after the other kids left for schools in Scotia Landing or Dorset. I just stayed in Mowat and nobody ever bothered me about it. Visitors—we called them visitors—who came up from Toronto and the States called it Algonquin but we just called it The Park. It was my home.

I was about seven when the mill shut down and the Gilmours left. When I was courting Katie Mattoonen, all that was left of Mowat was thirty dead acres where they'd dumped wood chips, sawdust, pine bark and bad logs into Canoe Lake. I'll bet the ground still springs back when you walk on it. They sold off the rest of the buildings and even the steel rails until nothing was left but the loggers' boarding house overlooking the chip yard. The Irishman put up a sign on it said MOWAT LODGE.

I got two box lunches from the Lodge kitchen and a loan of the new Chestnut. I loved that canoe. She was deep shady forest green canvas on the outside with a high gloss cedar inside that shone like a summer sunrise. The seats were caned and she sat sweet in the water, sixteen feet long with a tumblehome that made her look as slick as a speckled trout when you saw her side on. The Irishman said she was mine when I could afford it. I can still remember the feeling when I pushed her off from the dock, loaded with Katie and lunch and beers, like I was launching my whole life. The soft edge of the breeze, that smell of sow bugs and dead trees, new leaves and still frozen mud, the green blush of the maple buds and the black spikes of the evergreens on the western hills made you feel like you were inside some big church.

We paddled down past Wopomeo Island, past where they later found his body, and into Bonita Creek. For the daughter of the best guide in the southwest end of The Park Katie wasn't too handy with a paddle, but I could handle it all right. As long as we were in the breeze on Canoe Lake things were fine, but soon as we slipped into the shelter of the creek the wind dropped and the flies came up. Visitors call them Black Flies but we just call them flies. The damned things bite me but they don't raise welts like on most people. Matty said it's because I got so much fly poison in me already I'm immune, like him.

Katie sure wasn't immune. It wasn't like she didn't know about flies, but she started screaming when the first one bit her right where her black hair met the back of her white neck and she never stopped until I got us back where the breeze came up again. Her face looked like a red pumpkin, fat with fly bites, and she was so upset at what she thought she looked like she couldn't even talk. At sunset I sat out on the end of the dock, ate both lunches, drank both beers and thought about how pretty she looked even all puffed up.

At the Albion Hotel Matty told everyone The Painter said he'd lost all but two of fourteen dozen rolls of Kodak camera film when he tipped right in the middle of the damned lake because the flies got to him. He must have told everyone down south the same tall tale because it still gets told. Fourteen rolls maybe. Fourteen dozen? That would have been over 2,000 pictures. Laurence Dalton did the math. No one believed it then, and you'd think over time such fibs would get old and turn into lies and get forgotten. But the opposite seems to be true. Lies get truer with age. People believe what they want to and that makes it true.

I first met The Painter the next summer in 1913, when he just showed up one day with a pal. Matty and Laurence Dalton were guiding a group of teachers up toward Burnt Island, but The Painter wanted to get sketching right away so the Irishman gave me the Chestnut and said I'd show them around. Two artists from Toronto, he told me, but later I heard one of them say he made over eleven dollars a week. I knew grown men—hard workers too—in Huntsville and Dorset who didn't make that much in a month, sometimes in a winter. I thought real artists lived in attics and never had no money at all.

The Painter seemed nice enough, a tall, kinda shy, good-looking fella. Twice my age at the time. Talked more than he needed to but he had a twinkle in his eye and a pretty good handshake. But he sure couldn't work a canoe even though he'd convinced his pals he knew what he was doing. This one kept asking him questions about paddling and about The Park and he'd answer right off as if he knew, which he didn't.

With me in the Chestnut and them in the red canoe we worked our way around the lake every day for four days. The Painter kept slapping and swearing at the flies and telling me to take them here and there and asking me where could they find an old bent tree or a broke-down beaver dam to draw. He seemed more interested in the ugly stuff than the beautiful places that's everywhere around. I figured that's what experienced artists do, but when his pal said they'd bought their first paint kits just the year before, I didn't know what to think. So I just kept quiet. Anyways, they talked as if I wasn't there and seemed to think I didn't see how pretty everything was, being from Mowat and all. That bothered me, I remember, but I just paddled and watched for deadheads, them logs that point up from the lake bottom and hide just under the surface. They're quiet and invisible, but they'll rip through a canoe faster than a buck knife through a doe.

In the end it didn't matter whether they took photos, drew pictures or just gawked at the scenery, because they flipped her again. The Painter was in the stern of their canoe and I was sitting off to port so if they missed the dock they'd nudge me and slow down. It's a trick Laurence Dalton taught me. The Painter was changing paddle sides so much and yelling at his buddy that they rocked the same side together and that put them both in the water. I went after the friend who couldn't swim and the Irishman threw a line to The Painter. Four days of sketches sank clear to the bottom, but it wasn't worth getting hurt diving with all that mill trash under the dock. Matty's cousin's youngest boy from Trout Creek drownded when he got his shirt caught diving under there.

After supper I sat The Painter down on the Lodge dock with his butt over near the edge and I showed him the J-stroke, where you draw the paddle back 'til you get to the end and then tack on a little inside curve to straighten yourself out. Keeps you pointed where you're going even if you're alone. No thrashing around. No changing sides. Quiet. Once he figured it out, he slapped his thigh hard and howled like a hound and hugged me until it hurt. I heard he filled up some kind of a tank with water at his work and showed everyone the J-stroke, like someone who'd discovered a new thing and had to tell everybody about it. Like when Laurence Dalton's mother found Jesus over in Kearney. He was always a better talker than a paddler or a woodsman or a fisherman or whatever he wished he was—maybe than an artist for all I know. But he never came up in the winter when the place is so damned pretty and clean and sweet you'd crack your lips when you smiled just from breathing it in your nose.

The next summer he came back full of selling a painting for $250. I felt a sort of discomfort now that this picture was somewhere where people who'd never been to The Park could see it. His Park didn't look like The Park, leastwise not like my Park. Like he'd told another lie to a lot of people who didn't know any better.

Matty Mattoonen and Laurence Dalton weren't too pleased that The Painter asked for me again, but from then on it was always me he hired. He'd usually bring a pal, some close-shaved fella he'd filled full of tales about a northern paradise that the folks who lived there couldn't see. I actually heard him say that to a fella called Andy who was all full of the scenery over near the top end of Georgian Bay where he said the white quartz grew right out of the ground. We had white quartz in The Park too but we didn't go telling visitors where to find it.

We got to know each other a little better, but I can't say I got to like him any more. I finally got him to portage away from the crowds, and we'd paddle up Little Joe to Tepee and Littledoe to camp at Blackbear. I did all the work, from setting up the tent to cooking the meals and tying the food up so the bears couldn't get at it. He'd just stare off into the distance, thinking about paintings I guess. Sometimes he'd bring a little mandolin with him and sing songs after supper when I'd finished the dishes and built the fire back up. His voice was nice, I'll give him that, but some nights he'd drink more than a man ought to and that'd bring out a black temper. I seen him toss his whole paint kit into the bushes and then stomp off into the dark. In the morning he'd fish everything out of the forest and spend the whole day trying to fix the wood case where he'd broke it. He seemed to like fishing more than painting, which was fine with me, except he wasn't much good at that either. I showed him lures and lines and flies and talked about trout, especially the Lakers with their sharp-cut vee tails and how they liked it deep down in the cold water. Every time I caught a mess of fish he'd arrange them on a pan or on the grass or even hang them from a damned tent pole and take pictures of them. Maybe he told his pals he caught them. Don't matter. They were just fish.

I'd cleaned them and cooked them. For a man who said he liked the bush, he had an odd attitude about wildlife. Where'd he think food came from anyway? He got all upset when I snared a beaver and he wouldn't look when I butchered him or even eat any when

I cooked him up. Fatty things, but food when you're hungry and the weather's getting colder. Make a dog's coat shine.

I spent that winter reading up to be a Ranger, all about fire sighting and fighting, about how wildfires flare up with just the right amount of heat and grass and no one around and bang—you had a natural fire that could level an acre a minute. Park Ranger was the only real job besides guiding for me. Guiding didn't pay regular and the Irishman's wife told me I didn't have the temperment to wait on tables. If that meant I didn't like doing it, she'd have been right. She didn't like me much.

The news in the papers and on the radio that year was mostly about the Great War which seemed awful far away from The Park, except there were men up at Sim's Pit guarding the trains, so I guess it wasn't that far away. Katie Mattoonen asked me if I was gonna sign up in a manner that made me think real hard about it. With her to come home to you'd make damned sure you lived through it. She told me Russell and Laurence Dalton had signed up and her sister Doris' husband Jaako. She said it like they were already heroes, without a mention that there was no work for them at home anyway. I told her I'd think about it, but I thought more about her than the war.

The Painter came back in 1915 after the flies had gone, which showed he was learning something. He'd sold another painting to the Government in Ottawa. Sold another piece of The Park. He'd quit his paying job and some eye doctor was giving him money just to paint, which I thought kind of strange. Not a lot of money. He was always broke, bumming drinks from the Irishman and cash from everyone he met. Now he wanted to see The Park from higher up, said the view from the lake level didn't inspire him anymore. I took some offence to that. When he'd tried painting over at his eye doctor's place on Georgian Bay he came running back to The Park pretty quick, didn't he? We'd hike up to where the trees crowned and on the way he'd sketch and paint some views and hang the papers on trees to dry them off. Then we'd collect them on our way back to the canoe. Sometimes animals would bother them. One time, coming down a steep trail above Blackbear, we found one picture with a pile of bear shit right on top of it. I thought he'd have one of his artistic fits but he just laughed and said the bear was probably the smartest critic he'd come across.

I didn't pass the Ranger tests. They said I knew The Park backwards all right and how to survive year round but I didn't do so good on the distance math and I couldn't spell worth a damn. Matty said that was bullshit, that he knew Rangers who could add things and write good who couldn't find their way to the Albion Hotel, but that didn't change anything. That's what made me sign up. When I told The Painter he said he wanted to sign up too but they wouldn't take him. Once he told me it was because he'd had bad lungs as a youngster. Another time he told me he'd hurt his toe in a football match and they wouldn't take him because of his feet. I said his feet seemed fine to me—we hiked 20 miles on a good day—and he agreed, swearing a little and wishing he could go to war. I found out that was a stupid wish.

There was quite a party at the Lodge the night before I left. It was late August and cool, my favourite time of year in The Park. There were no bugs, the days were warm, and the Lake Trout would soon come back up from deep water. In a couple of weeks the leaves would begin to bleed colours even them Kodachrome postcards can't show right. The Painter's success, or his talking about it, had brought a bunch more artist types up to Mowat, as well as more visitors than the place had ever seen, so the winging was a big one. They'd hired up a band from Huntsville and The Painter and the Irishman tried to get me to dance but I wasn't having any because I didn't know how. I just sat there beside Katie, touching hands when Matty wasn't looking, enjoying attention like I'd never had before and half glad

I was leaving Mowat the next day. Boy, she looked like something that night, I'll tell you.

When the bonfire burned down most folks went to bed. We were all pretty drunk. The Painter pulled out his mandolin and played a song or two about being lonely and away from home and not being cared for. I was falling asleep when The Painter and Katie took a walk beyond the campfire, into the dark. I never really thought about that until I was on the train to Toronto the next day. That's when I felt most lonely of all. That's when I felt the most hurt heart I could ever remember, then or since.

I never talked much about the Great War then and I don't now. I ended up in the goddamned mud with the Canadian Corps on Easter Monday, 1917. Four days later we took Vimy Ridge, 120 yards high, about the same as that granite ridge just west of where Mowat used to be. I got shot in the right thigh and fell face down in a muck bog that went on to the horizon. I was dreaming I was a pure white otter diving down deep in the cool clean water of a two-loon lake when somebody flipped me onto my back. Saved my life. I would have drownded right there.

I came home in July with a silver medal, a pension, a limp and an Army-issue cane. At first not much seemed changed. The fat deer flies swarmed around my head just out of range like always. The hot purple and burnt cloud sunset shadows on the lakes were the same ones I'd been thinking about all the time I was away. Maybe they were even more beautiful for that. The Lodge was bigger and packed with more visitors than ever. The chip yard was growing in fast with weedy poplars and runt balsams. From the dock I saw The Painter zigzagging his way up Canoe Lake like an amateur, but it wasn't until he got close that I saw he had my Chestnut, except he'd painted her grey. He shouted my name and put his arms around me like a bear and hugged me and banged on my back like I was a relative or something. He talked about all the paintings he had done and sold, how all his pals were coming up, how The Park had been discovered. All I could smell was his shirt and his sweat and all I could feel was my head getting hotter and hotter, 'til my collar was soaking and my neck burned like a fuse in the cold afternoon wind. He didn't even ask me where I'd been.

Things weren't at all the same, I saw. Matty said The Painter had made some money guiding Lodge guests around Canoe in the Chestnut. He'd passed his Park Ranger easy, said the Irishman, and had been fire spotting over on the east end side all spring. They all seemed prouder of him than me. And I was from here. And I'd come home from away. It was like he'd taken over my Park while I was gone. Never mind he couldn't paddle or find his own way to Blackbear. Never mind he couldn't catch a fish or trap a meal. Never mind he didn't go overseas. The Irishman's wife watched me real close when she said Katie Mattoonen married Russell Dalton the minute he'd come back all gassed up from France. Laurence Dalton hadn't come back at all and I wished I hadn't either.

I know it don't make no sense at all when you sit back and study it. It all blew up without warning. Like white wildfire. It just blazed up when I was being hugged on that dock. Nobody saw it coming, leastwise me. He had my canoe. He'd walked out of that campfire light with my girl. He was guiding. He'd made Ranger. He'd taken my friends and my family and my town. And with his goddamned paintings he'd stole my Park and sold it away for money. With his fucking paint brushes and smelly little tubes of paint and his foul temper and his dull drawings and his dirty goddamned gobs of colour, he'd taken my Park and made it something ugly and lonely and thick and threatening and dangerous. He'd stomped right into my church and he'd stepped on my heart and he'd upset my soul and he didn't even see it and he didn't even give a sweet goddamn. While we stood there on that dock, him smelling like fire and hugging me and welcoming me home and waving over my head saying "Look who's here with his little silver medal," I knew I'd kill the bastard. And when the Irishman told me at supper the Ranger had seen a whopper of a Laker up by the Joe Lake portage I knew just how to do it.

I never thought twice after that. If I told The Painter where and how he could catch the biggest Laker around, he'd believe me without even thinking about why I'd bother to tell him. He'd only think about himself, local hero, big time artist with a way in the woods and the champeen taker of the biggest trout on the lake. I told him the biggest fish on the lake was in that little inlet that runs west off the northern tip of Wapomeo Island, and that dew worms fished deep would do it in the early afternoon. Weight the line two feet from the hook, I told him, then let it out until it hits bottom and then reel it in just an inch or so. Then leave it. Quiet. His eyes opened wide when I told him, like a little kid's at the first tug from a sunfish.

In the morning I watched from the point while he and the Ranger fished the Joe Lake portage and caught nothing. I watched him paddle my Chestnut back to the dock, go into the Lodge and come out hiding a tin of worms, looking back over his shoulder like the thief he was. I knew then I had him like you know when you've clean lip-hooked a fine fighting fish. You just feel it. You're no longer equals. I watched him paddle down to the inlet and disappear west behind the pink granite ridge.

When I glided in he was near the south shore shallows across from the point, not at all where I'd told him to fish. He was using copper line, which I'd taught him to use deep because Lake Trout'll bite through hair and silk, but he'd missed a cast badly and had wrapped it all around his ankle. I felt an acid flush fast into my gut, and a carbon taste on the back of my tongue like the stink of a short circuit. I hit him hard with my paddle, right in the head, right over his left eye. Blood shot out his ear when he fell face down into the water. He'd been so intent on unravelling the line he didn't hear me;

a J-stroke makes no noise if you know what you're doing. I sat in the summer sun with my paddle dripping water and blood and I watched him, unconscious, suck in the reedy black water and drown. I don't think he even saw me, but I hope he did.

I jumped into the shallows and pulled the Chestnut into shore. He had some bread and bacon in a canvas bag which I stuffed in the crevice of the bow. I made sure the little portage paddle was fixed to the forward seat and I lashed the other two paddles to make it look like he'd carried them in from somewhere else. I threw his small axe high into the deep water of the inlet and I still remember how the sun caught it like the glint off a white quartz outcrop. When I tipped his canoe over, I could see some green where the rocks had scraped off the grey paint. I towed his body and the canoe out into the lake and then let both float free, both face down. I threw his gear into the water and watched as the cork rod handles fought to float, then gave up and sank in the deep channel. Then I paddled back to Mowat for supper.

Oh I followed the news. I have for years now. I heard how the fishing line around his ankle was a big mystery. Some fool said he'd probably caught the big trout and wrapped the line around his ankle to hold it. Another thought he'd sprained his ankle on a portage and wrapped fishing line around it for support. His city friends all said he couldn't have drownded himself because he was such a damned good paddler. Others said he might have been killed because of a woman, even though he was forty and no one had ever known him to say more than three words to one, except maybe Katie Mattoonen in the dark. Some even said he'd committed suicide because his paintings weren't selling. No one seemed to remember that he'd only been painting for six goddamned years. Christ, by then I'd been paddling for twenty.

His lies bothered me then, but now I'm old and I don't give a shit anymore. I got the Chestnut back when it was found and after a while

I painted her green again. I lived in The Park on my Army money until I got hurt up on Sunbeam and was found by a long-haired kid and his girlfriend. She hardly had anything on. The Lodge burned down, got rebuilt and burned again. I outlived them all, lived long enough to see another batch of local boys go to another goddamned war and not come back the same. Or at all.

Bullshit wins the day is all I've learned from it. Everyone still thinks he was a fine paddler and woodsman and artist, even though it was only him told people that's what he was. There's a pile of granite rocks to his memory on the point where I watched him paddle past. And forty years after they found him dead they named a lake after the bastard—changed it from Blackbear. They never named no lake for Matty Mattoonen. Or Laurence Dalton who got killed. No one remembers them.

If I hadn't killed The Painter he'd be forgotten too.

Safe Enough

by

LEE CHILD

WOLFE WAS A CITY BOY. From birth his world had been iron and concrete, first one city block, then two, then four, then eight. Trees had been visible only from the roof of his building, far away across the East River, as remote as legends. Until he was twenty-eight years old the only mown grass he had ever seen was the outfield at Yankee Stadium. He was oblivious to the chlorine taste of city water, and to him the roar of traffic was the same thing as absolute tranquil silence.

Now he lived in the country.

Anyone else would have called it the suburbs, but there were broad spaces between dwellings, and no way of knowing what your neighbour was cooking other than getting invited to dinner, and there was insect life in the yards, and wild deer, and the possibility of mice in the basement, and drifts of leaves in the fall, and electricity came through wires slung on poles and water came from wells.

To Wolfe, that was the country.

That was the wild frontier.

That was the end of a long and winding road.

The road had started winding twenty-three years earlier in a Bronx public elementary school. Back in those rudimentary days a boy was marked early. Hooligan, wastrel, artisan, genius—the label was slapped firmly in place and it stuck forever. Wolfe had been reasonably well behaved and had managed shop and arithmetic pretty well, so he was stuck in the artisan category and expected to grow up to be a plumber or an electrician or an air conditioning guy. He was expected to find a sponsor in the appropriate local and get admitted to an apprentice-ship and then work for forty-five years. Which is precisely how it turned out for Wolfe. He went the electrician route and was ten years into his allotted forty-five when it happened.

What happened was that the construction boom in the suburbs finally overwhelmed the indigenous supply of father-and-son electri-cal contractors. That was all they had up there. Small guys, family firms, one-truck operations, Mom doing the invoices. Same for the local roofers and plumbers and drywall people. Demand outran supply. But the developers had bucks to make and couldn't tolerate delay. So they swallowed their pride and sent flyers down to the city union halls, and followed them with minivans, pickup at seven in the morning, back in time for dinner. They found it easy to compete on wages. City budgets were stalled.

Wolfe was not the first to sign up, but he wasn't the last. Every morning at seven o'clock he would climb into a Dodge Caravan full of stuff belonging to some suburban foreman's kids. A bunch of other city guys would climb in behind him. They would stay silent and morose through the one-hour trip, but they watched out the windows with a degree of curiosity. Some of them were turned out early in a manicured town full of quarter-acre lots. Some of them stayed in until the trees thickened up and they hit the north of the county.

Wolfe was put to work on the last stop up the line.

Anyone who had seen a little more geography than Wolfe would have pegged the place correctly as mildly undulating terrain covered with hundred-year-old second-growth forestation and a few glacial boulders, with some minor streams and some small ponds. Wolfe thought it was the Rocky Mountains. To him, it was unbelievably dramatic. Birds sang and chipmunks darted and there was grey lichen on the rocks and tangled riots of vines everywhere.

His work site was a stick-built wooden house going up on a nine-acre lot. Every conceivable thing was different from the city. There was raw mud under his feet. Power came in on a cable as thick as his wrist that was spliced off another looping between two tarred poles on the shoulder of the road. The new feed was terminated at a meter and a breaker box screwed to a ply board that was set upright in the earth like a gravestone. It was a two-hundred-amp supply. It ran underground in a gravelled trench the length of the future driveway, which was about as long as the Grand Concourse. Then it came out in the future basement, through a patched wound in the concrete foundation.

Then it was Wolfe's to deal with.

He worked alone most of the time. Drywall crews were scarce. Nobody was slated to show up until he was finished. Then they would blitz the Sheetrock job and move on. So Wolfe was a small cog in a big dispersed machine. He was happy enough about that. It was easy work. And pleasant. He liked the smell of the raw lumber. He liked the ease of drilling wooden studs with an augur instead of fighting through brick or concrete with a hammer. He liked the way he could stand up most of the time, instead of crawling. He liked the fresh cleanliness of the site. Better than poking around in piles of old rat shit.

He grew to like the area too.

Every day he brought a bag lunch from a deli at home. At first he ate in what was going to be the garage, sitting on a plank. Then he took to venturing out and sitting on a rock. Then he found a better rock, near a stream. Then he found a place across the stream with two rocks, one like a table and the other like a chair.

Then he found a woman.

She was walking through the woods, fast. Vines whipped at her legs. He saw her, but she didn't see him. She was preoccupied. Angry, or upset. She looked like a spirit of the countryside. A goddess of the forest. She was tall, she was straight, she had untamed straw-blond hair, she wore no makeup. She had what magazines call bone structure. She had blue eyes and pale delicate hands.

Later, from the foreman, Wolfe learned that the lot he was working on had been her land. She had sold nine of thirty acres for development. Wolfe also learned that her marriage was in trouble. Local scuttlebutt said that her husband was an asshole. He was a Wall Street guy who commuted on Metro North. Never home, and when he was he gave her a hard time. Story was he had tried to stop her selling the nine acres, but the land was hers. Story was they fought all the time, in that tight-ass half-concealed way that respectable people use. The husband had been heard to say *I'll f-ing kill you* to her. She was a little more buttoned-up, but the story was she had said it right back.

Suburban gossip was amazingly extensive. Where Wolfe was from, you didn't need gossip. You heard everything through the walls.

They gave Wolfe time and a half to work Saturdays and slipped him big bills to run phone lines and cable. Being a union man, he shouldn't have done it. But there were going to be modems, and a media room, and five bedroom phone extensions sharing three lines. Plus fax. Plus a DSL option. So he took the money and did the work.

He saw the woman most days.

She didn't see him.

He learned her routine. She had a green Volvo wagon, and he would see it pass the bottom of the new driveway when she went to the store. One day he saw it go by and he downed tools and walked through the woods and stepped over the property line onto her land. Walked where she had walked. The trees were dense, but after about twenty yards he came out on a broad lawn that led up to her house. The first time, he stopped there, right on the edge.

The second time, he went a little farther.

By the fifth time, he had been all over her property. He had explored everything. He had taken his shoes off and padded through her kitchen. She didn't lock her door. Nobody did, in the suburbs. It was a badge of distinction. "We never lock our doors," they all said, with a little laugh.

More fool them.

Wolfe finished the furnace line in the new basement and started on the first floor. Every day he took his lunch to the twin rocks. One time-and-a-half Saturday he saw the woman and her husband together. They were on their lawn, fighting. Not physically. Verbally. They were striding up and down the grass in the hot sunlight, and Wolfe saw them between tree branches like they were on a stage under a flashing stroboscope. Like disco. Fast sequential poses of anger and hurt. The guy was an asshole, for sure. Completely unreasonable, in Wolfe's estimation. The more he railed, the lovelier the woman looked. Like a martyr in a church window. Wounded, vulnerable, noble.

Then the asshole hit her.

It was a kind of girly roundhouse slap. Try that where Wolfe was from and your opponent would laugh for a minute before beating you to a pulp. But it worked well enough on the woman. The asshole was tall and fleshy and he got enough of his dumb bulk behind the blow to lift her off her feet and dump her on her back on the grass. She sat up, stunned. Disbelieving. There was a livid red mark on her cheek. She started to cry. Not tears of pain. Not even tears of rage. Just tears of sheer heartbroken sadness that whatever great things her life had promised, it had all come down to being dumped on her ass on her own back lawn, with four fingers and a thumb printed backwards on her face.

Soon after that it was the Fourth of July weekend and Wolfe stayed at home for four days.

WHEN THE DODGE CARAVAN brought him back again he saw a bunch of local cop cars coming down the road. From the woman's house, probably. No flashing lights. He glanced at them twice and started work. Second floor, three lighting circuits. Switched outlets and ceiling fixtures. Wall sconces in the bathrooms. But the whine of his augur must have told the woman he was there, because she came over to see him. First time she had actually laid eyes on him. As far as he knew. Certainly it was the first time they had talked.

She crunched her way over the driveway grit and leaned in past the plywood sheet that was standing in for the front door and called, "Hello?"

Wolfe heard her over the noise of the drill and clattered down the stairs. She had stepped inside the hallway. The light was behind her. It made a halo of her hair. She was wearing old jeans and a T-shirt. She was a vision of loveliness.

"I'm sorry to bother you," she said.

Her voice was like an angel's caress.

Wolfe said, "No bother."

"My husband has disappeared," she said.

"Disappeared?" Wolfe said.

"He wasn't home over the weekend and he isn't at work today."

Wolfe said nothing.

The woman said, "The police will come to see you. I'm here to apologize for that in advance. That's all, really."

But Wolfe could tell it wasn't.

"Why would the police come to see me?" he asked.

"I think they'll have to. I think that's how they do things. They'll probably want to know if you saw anything. Or heard any … disturbances."

The way she said *disturbances* was really a question, in real time, from her to him, not just a future prediction of what the cops might ask. As in, *Did you hear the disturbances? Did you? Or not?*

Wolfe said, "My name is Wolfe. I'm pleased to meet you."

The woman said, "I'm Mary. Mary Lovell."

Lovell. Like love, with two extra letters.

"Did you hear anything, Mr. Wolfe?"

"No," Wolfe said. "I'm just working here. Making a bit of noise myself."

"It's just that the police are being a bit … distant. I know that if a wife disappears, the police always suspect the husband. Until something is proven otherwise. I'm wondering if they're wondering the same kind of thing, but in reverse."

Wolfe said nothing.

"Especially if there have been disturbances," Mary Lovell said.

"I didn't hear anything," Wolfe said.

"Especially if the wife isn't very upset."

"Aren't you upset?"

"I'm a little sad. Sad that I'm happy."

SURE ENOUGH THE POLICE came by about two hours later. Two of them. Town cops, in uniform. Wolfe guessed the department wasn't big enough to carry detectives. The cops approached him politely and told him a long and rambling story that basically recapped the local gossip. Husband and wife on the outs, always fighting, famous for it.

They said upfront and man to man that if the wife had disappeared they'd have some serious questions for the husband. The other way around was unusual but not unknown and, frankly, the town was full of rumours. So, they asked, could Mr. Wolfe shed any light?

No, Mr. Wolfe said, he couldn't.

"Never seen them?" the first cop asked.

"I guess I've seen her," Wolfe said. "In her car, time to time. Leastways, I'm guessing it was her. Right direction."

"Green Volvo?"

"That was it."

"Never seen him?" the second cop asked.

"Never," Wolfe said. "I'm just here working."

"Ever heard anything?"

"Like what?"

"Like fights, or altercations."

"Not a thing."

The first cop said, "This is a guy who apparently walked away from a big career in the city. And guys don't do that. They get lawyers instead."

"What can I tell you?"

"We're just saying."

"Saying what?"

"The load bed on that Volvo is seven feet long, you put the seats down."

"So?"

"It would help us to hear that you didn't happen to look out the window and see that Volvo drive past with something maybe six-three long, maybe wrapped up in a rug or a sheet of plastic."

"I didn't."

"She's known to have uttered threats. Him too. I'm telling you, if she was gone, we'd be looking at him, for sure."

Wolfe said nothing.

The cop said, "Therefore we have to look at her. We have to be sensitive about equality. It's forced on us."

The cop looked at Wolfe one last time, working man to working man, appealing for class solidarity, hoping for a break.

But Wolfe just said, "I'm working here. I don't see things."

WOLFE SAW COP CARS up and down the road all day long. He didn't go home that night. He let the Dodge Caravan leave without him and went over to Mary Lovell's house.

He said, "I came by to see how you're doing."

She said, "They think I killed him."

She led him inside to the kitchen he had visited before.

She said, "They have witnesses who heard me make threats. But they were meaningless. Just things you say in fights."

"Everyone says those things," Wolfe said.

"But it's really his job they're worried about. They say nobody just walks away from a job like his. And they're right. And if somebody did, they'd use a credit card for a plane or a hotel. And he hasn't. So what's he doing? Using cash in a fleabag motel somewhere? Why would he do that? That's what they're harping on."

Wolfe said nothing.

Mary Lovell said, "He's just disappeared. It's impossible to explain."

Wolfe said nothing.

Mary Lovell said, "I would suspect myself too. I really would."

"Is there a gun in the house?" Wolfe asked.

"No," Mary said.

"Kitchen knives all accounted for?"

"Yes."

"So how do they think you did it?"

"They haven't said."

"They've got nothing," Wolfe said.

Then he went quiet.

Mary said, "What?"

Wolfe said, "I saw him hit you."

"When?"

"Before the holidays. I was in the woods, you were on the lawn."

"You *watched* us?"

"I saw you. There's a difference."

"Did you tell the police?"

"No."

"Why not?"

"I wanted to talk to you first."

"About what?"

"I wanted to ask you a question."

"What question?"

"Did you kill him?"

There was a tiny pause, hardly there at all, and then Mary Lovell said, "No."

IT STARTED THAT NIGHT. They felt like conspirators. Mary Lovell was the kind of suburban avant-garde bohemian that didn't let herself dismiss an electrician from the Bronx out of hand. And Wolfe had nothing against upscale women. Nothing at all.

WOLFE NEVER WENT HOME AGAIN. The first three months were tough. Taking a new lover five days after her husband was last seen alive made things worse for Mary Lovell. Obviously. Much worse. The rumour mill started up full blast and the cops never left her alone. But she got through it. At night, with Wolfe, she was fine. The tiny seed of doubt that she knew had to be in his mind bound her to him. He never mentioned it. He was always unfailingly loyal. It made her feel committed to him, unquestioningly, like a fact of life. Like she was a princess and had been promised to someone at birth. That she liked him just made it better.

AFTER THREE MONTHS the cops moved on, mentally. The Lovell husband's file gathered dust as an unsolved case. The rumour mill quieted. In a year it was ancient history. Mary and Wolfe got along fine. Life was good. Wolfe set up as a one-man contractor. Worked for the local developers out of a truck that Mary bought for him. She did the invoices.

IT SOURED before their third Christmas. Finally Mary admitted to herself that beyond the bohemian attraction, her electrician from the Bronx was a little … boring. He didn't *know* anything. And his family was a pack of wild animals. And the fact that she was bound to him by the tiny seed of doubt that had to be in his mind became a source of resentment, not charm. She felt that far from being clandestine co-conspirators they were now cell mates in a prison constructed by her long-forgotten husband.

For his part Wolfe was getting progressively more and more irritated by her. She was so damn snooty about everything. So smug, so superior. She didn't like baseball. And she said even if she did, she wouldn't root for the Yankees. They just bought everything. Like she didn't?

He began to sympathize vaguely with the long-forgotten husband. One time he replayed the slap on the lawn in his mind. The long sweep of the guy's arm, the arc of his hand. He imagined the rush of air on his own palm and the sharp sting that would come as contact was made.

Maybe she had deserved it.

One time, face-to-face with her in the kitchen, he found his own arm moving in the same way. He checked it inside a quarter-inch. Mary never noticed. Maybe she was shaping up to hit him. It seemed only a matter of time.

The third Christmas was when it fell apart. Or to be accurate, the aftermath of the third Christmas. The holiday itself was okay. Just. Afterward she was prissy. As usual. In the Bronx you had fun and then you threw the tree on the sidewalk. But she always waited until January sixth and planted the tree in the yard.

"Shame to waste a living thing," she would say.

The trees she made him buy had roots. He had never before seen a Christmas tree with roots. To him, it was all wrong. It spoke of foresight, and concern for the long-term, and some kind of guilt-ridden self-justification. Like you were permitted to have fun only if you did the right thing afterward. It wasn't like that in Wolfe's world. In Wolfe's world, fun was fun. No before, and no after.

Planting a tree to her was cutesy. To him it was a back-breaking hour digging in the freezing cold.

They fought about it, of course. Long, loud, and hard. Within seconds it was all about class and background and culture. Furious insults were thrown. The air grew thick with them. They kept on until they were physically too tired to continue. Wolfe was shaken. She had reached in and touched a nerve. Touched his core: *No woman should speak to a man like that.* He knew it was an ignoble feeling. He knew it was wrong, out of date, too traditional for words.

But he was what he was.

He looked at her and in that moment he knew he hated her. He found his gloves and wrapped himself up in his down coat and seized the tree by a branch and hurled it out the back door. Detoured via the garage and seized a shovel. Dragged the tree behind him to a spot at the edge of the lawn, under the shade of a giant maple, where the snow was thin and the damn Christmas tree would be sure to die. He kicked leaf litter and snow out of his way and plunged the shovel into the earth. Hurled clods deep into the woods. Cut maple roots with vicious stabs. After ten minutes sweat was rolling down his back. After fifteen minutes the hole was two feet deep.

After twenty minutes he saw the first bone.

He fell to his knees. Swept dirt away with his hands. The thing was dirty white, long, shaped like the kind of thing you gave a dog in a cartoon show. There were stringy dried ligaments attached to it and rotted cotton cloth surrounding it.

Wolfe stood up. Turned slowly and stared at the house. Walked toward it. Stopped in the kitchen. Opened his mouth.

"Come to apologize?" Mary said.

Wolfe turned away. Picked up the phone.

Dialed 911.

THE LOCALS CALLED the state troopers. Mary was kept under some kind of unofficial house arrest in the kitchen until the excavation was completed. A state lieutenant showed up with a search warrant. One of his men pulled an old credenza away from the garage wall and found a hammer behind it. A carpentry tool. Dried blood and old hair were still clearly visible on it. It was bagged up and carried out to the yard. The profile of its head exactly matched the hole punched through the skull they had found in the ground.

At that point Mary Lovell was arrested for the murder of her husband.

THEN SCIENCE TOOK OVER. Dental, blood, and DNA tests proved the remains to be those of the husband. No question about that. It was the husband's blood and hair on the hammer too. No question about that either. Mary's fingerprints were on the hammer's handle. Twenty-three points of similarity, more than enough for the locals, the state police, and the FBI all put together.

THEN LAWYERS TOOK OVER. The county DA loved the case to bits. To put a middle-class white woman away would prove his impartial even-handedness. Mary got a lawyer, the friend of a friend. He was good, but overmatched. Not by the DA. By the weight of evidence. Mary wanted to plead not guilty, but he persuaded her to say yes to manslaughter. Emotional turmoil, temporary loss of reason, everlasting regret and remorse. So one day in late spring Wolfe sat in the courtroom and watched her go down for a minimum ten years. She looked at him only once during the whole proceeding.

Then Wolfe went back to her house.

HE LIVED THERE alone for many years. He kept on working and did his own invoices. He grew to really love the solitude and the silence. Sometimes he drove down to the stadium, but when parking hit twenty bucks he figured his Bronx days were over. He bought a big-screen TV. Did his own cable work, of course. Watched the games at home. Sometimes after the last out he would sit in the dark and review the case in his head. Cops, lawyers, dozens of them. They had done a pretty thorough job between them.

But they had missed two vital questions.

One: With her pale delicate hands, how was Mary Lovell accustomed to handling hammers and shovels? Why did the local cops right at the beginning not see angry red blisters all over her palms? And two: How did Wolfe know exactly where to start digging the hole for that damn Christmas tree? Right after the fight? Aren't cops supposed to hate coincidences?

But all in all, Wolfe figured he was safe enough.

The Meeting

by

MARGIE ORFORD

TWENTY MINUTES' DRIVE EAST from her city apartment and Table Mountain was a blue cut-out beneath the bleached summer sky. Clare Hart turned off the freeway, the off-ramp sinking her into Khayelitsha, Cape Town's teeming shadow-city sprawling unmapped across the sand dunes south of the airport. The houses, makeshift cubes of corrugated iron and wood roofed with black plastic, housed half a million people, maybe a million.

No one was counting.

The road looped under a bridge where shacks sprouted under the concrete ribs holding the flyover aloft. A woman emptying water into the tub of pink geraniums at her front door raised her hand in greeting. Clare flashed her lights in return. A group of small boys huddled together throwing dice abandoned their game to race alongside her car, dropping back one by one. The one who fell back last turned back doing a footballer's victory lap, arms outstretched like wings, to join his companions under the bridge.

The main road was thronged with people and vehicles, lined with small plywood stores fringed with onions and oranges. On the counters, enamel bowls were piled with tomatoes. Withered apples had been counted out, two or three per bag. Severed sheep's heads grinned beneath a cloud of buzzing flies while the stallholder haggled with a customer. The wind whipped at women's skirts as they called out to passers-by, luring them with freshly baked *vetkoek* and offal sizzling above the coals. Men loitering near the bass-thumping taxis bellowed their routes, waiting for enough passengers to warrant a trip.

Noise filled every crevice between the houses and pushed through the shatterproof windows of Clare's car as she inched forward. This would be her second meeting with Isaac Molweni. He had called her that morning, saying he had to see her today. Could she come straight after school came out? Could she bring the pictures?

The photographs were on the seat next to her. Isaac's careful directions *(left at the second set of lights, look for the traditional doctor's sign at the cul-de-sac, right where the vendors sell sun glasses, there was his school, opposite Shoprite)* were in the boot, tucked into her bag with the pathologist's report and her tape recorder.

A girl in a yellow sundress waited at the traffic light, a vetkoek in her hand. She split it, putting one half whole into her mouth.

The lights turned red.

Clare stopped.

The girl strolled across the road. She paused in front of Clare's car to greet a friend walking in the opposite direction, handing the other half of her cake to the toddler tied to her back. The child stared at Clare as he bit into it, transfixing her as his eyes widened with pleasure. The same limpid eyes as the bewildered child Clare had held on her lap last week in the Molwenis' two-roomed house; Lorna's relatives crowded quietly in the kitchen; the slouching boys in the street who had made way for her when she had arrived.

Lorna Molweni's son had curled his warm body into Clare's, retreating behind the curtain of her hair to lick the pink icing off his cupcake. There had been fifty people there, but nobody heard. Nobody saw this. Clare had stared at the grainy images of his mother's plump body laid out amongst the tea things. No police photographer had come, Isaac Molweni had explained, so he had taken these pictures with his cell phone. For evidence. So that Dr. Hart could help him. Then Isaac had pieced together for Clare what had happened to his sister.

LORNA HAD HER hair braided.

Lorna went to a tavern.

Lorna did not come home.

He, Isaac, had gone to look for Lorna because Lorna had to eat, take her medicine.

He found Lorna naked behind the toilets of the shebeen.

Lorna's eyes were swollen shut.

Lorna's belly had a bloody AIDS ribbon knifed onto it.

Lorna's body had been split between her legs. Look, Doctor, here is the picture I took of my sister.

There had been eight men, the people who saw nothing had told him.

Lorna had breath to say two names. Jackson, Sizwe.

Lorna did not know the other six.

THE LIGHTS turned green.

A mini-bus taxi swooped in front of Clare, the bass reverberating through her chest. The girl in the yellow dress got in, the door sliding shut on her laughter. The truck driver behind Clare leaned on his hooter and she jerked forward, turning left, away from his gesticulated obscenities. The hand-painted sign pointed down the road offering HAIR GHANA STYLE. BRAIDS FOR THE LAYDEES, FOR THE GENTS.

Not Dr. Khoza's fifty-rand traditional cures for bad luck, impotence and AIDS.

There was a little pop below Clare's heart. She had turned too soon and the road was too narrow to turn back.

She drove on until the tar petered out into an open lot where a recent fire had reduced scores of shacks to blackened stumps and twisted pieces of metal. Ahead of her, shacks crowded around a tangle of tracks. The brightly coloured washing snapping on lines marked one handkerchief of space off from another. Two goats nosed around smouldering rubbish piled against a fence. No cheerful women doing washing here. Clare went left, thinking it would U-turn her back onto the main road.

The road narrowed, slowing her to a crawl.

Clare stopped outside a dilapidated shack to get her bearings. She didn't see anyone except the half-naked child leaning against the doorpost watching her, a thumb plugged into her mouth. A scrawny bitch lay in the dust on the pavement, new-born puppies heaped against her belly. Kwaito thumped its sullen beat from the speaker hooked on the lopsided sign of the Nice Time Tavern. A tattered red umbrella provided a puddle of shade for three men sitting on upturned blue crates, quarts of Black Label on the plastic table. An old woman filling her bucket at the communal tap kept a wary eye on them.

A man unpeeled from a wall across the street, his hands in his pockets, his hat pulled low. Clare calculated how many manoeuvres it would take to turn the car around. How long it would take. Too many. Too long.

Another pop.

In her heart this time.

The door where the child stood snapped shut, the little girl pulled inside by a slender arm. The sharp sound took Clare's eyes off the man for a second.

HE WAS STANDING at her window, both hands up, palms pink, open against his tight red T-shirt. She looked from his hands to his face, at the thin scar that threaded his left eyebrow, across the rounded cheek. A trace of childhood lingered in his eyes. Clare put him at fifteen, maybe sixteen. He tossed Clare a smile, making a tumbling motion with his hands, motioning her to open up. A vein pulsed in the hollow of his throat. She ignored the machine gun pop pop popping in her heart and cracked open the window.

"You're wrong here, *sisi*," he said.

"I know," said Clare, her mouth dry. The old woman, bent by the weight of the bucket on her head, scurried away down an alley.

"Where are you going?" he asked.

"To meet someone near Shoprite." It was close enough to the truth. Isaac's school was very close by.

"You turned too soon. I show you the way out." His eyes were on the road behind Clare's car.

Clare saw movement in the corner of her eye. One of the men from the shebeen was sauntering towards her down the track. Another of the drinkers stood, drained his beer and placed the bottle on the table, his right hand sliding with practised smoothness towards his trouser pocket.

The boy was at the other side of the car.

Clare opened the door.

The boy was inside. He pressed down the lock with his left elbow. The envelope of photographs was on his lap, his slender fingers curled around Lorna's name. He angled the sun visor so he could watch the street behind them in the vanity mirror. The smell of him—Vinolia soap, wood smoke, adrenalin—filled the car.

"Drive," said the boy. The men from the shebeen had fanned out. The one on the right broke into a slow trot. He was closing in. "Now!"

Clare slipped the car into first, churning the wheels in the sand. The wheels bit and she breathed out, driving fast between the shacks. The strands of barbed wire in front of each dwelling were so close to the car that the hairs on her arms rose. The man from the shebeen stopped and urinated, aiming at the dog. She slunk off fast, scattering puppies. The other two fell back, returning to their beers outside the shebeen.

"Turn here." Clare turned. The street was wider. Schoolboys in grey shorts and white shirts trailing bags behind them parted to let the car through.

"What's your name?" asked Clare.

"Andile." The boy pointed again. "And here, turn." They were back on the main road. Clare wound down her window and the comforting sounds of the busy street enfolded her. She pulled over and the boy got out.

"Two robots." The boy pointed ahead. "You turn left at the shopping centre."

"Thank you, Andile," said Clare.

"You're here for Lorna." It was not a question.

"You knew her?"

"I saw her." Andile traced the loop of the AIDS ribbon on the window with his forefinger, his shirt colouring it crimson through the pale dust.

"Lorna?"

"I see them." His voice just above a whisper.

"Jackson, Sizwe?" asked Clare. A taxi throbbed past and his answer was lost.

"The others?"

"You must be careful, *sisi*." He handed her the brown envelope containing Isaac's photographs and took off, his blade of a body disappearing between the fruit stalls. Clare leafed quickly through the enlarged prints till she found the only wide shot of the shebeen.

The Nice Time Tavern.

Clare slid her hands off the steering wheel, wiped her sweaty palms on her jeans and drew a deep breath. She leapt out of her car, activating the alarm at twenty paces. Fifty paces and she had squeezed between the stalls where the boy had disappeared, ignoring the shouts of the hawkers. Behind the little shops, the road forked into two dusty tracks. Clare slowed for a second to orientate herself. To the right a flash of red. She sprinted towards it, turning the corner where Andile had turned. He was leaning over a fence, trying to catch his breath. He took off when he saw her but Clare was fast. She was gaining. At the next corner she was on him, one slim, strong arm coiled hard on his throat, pulling his bony body tight against hers.

"Tell me what you did." Clare's voice harsh from running. He twisted in her grip and she pulled his left arm high between his shoulder blades. He gasped. The women who had abandoned their stalls to follow pressed in around them, yelling at the boy in Xhosa.

"I helped you, *sisi*," he said.

The crowd was swelling, volleying questions and comments over their heads. In the distance a siren wailed.

"Because of Lorna?" Clare's mouth was close to his ear.

Andile's heart thudded against Clare's chest. "I did nothing."

"I know," she said.

Clare's phone beeped in her back pocket. Two o'clock. She was late for her meeting.

"That'll be Isaac Molweni," she said. "Lorna's brother." Andile stood dead still and she loosened her grip on his neck. "This is your chance."

He nodded. Clare let his arm go and Andile turned to face her, rubbing his shoulder to get the blood flowing again. A small boy darted forward and handed him his hat. Andile pulled it down low, tilting his face up.

"I will tell Isaac." Andile looked Clare in the eye. "I will tell him what I saw."

The Weeping Time

by

MAUREEN JENNINGS

MASTER JAMES KENNETT had hardly reached the doorstep of the farmhouse when the door opened. Sarah, the old man's granddaughter, greeted him with a smile, but her voice was anxious.

"Come in. He hath been asking for you."

"Beg pardon mistress, the path was icy and we had to go with care."

He followed her into the kitchen, which was hot and so redolent with the smell of roasting mutton that the grease settled in a film on his lips. A small girl was turning a spit on the wide hearth, watched by two scrawny hounds.

"Warm yourself first," said Sarah. "And if it please you, sup with us afterward."

James went to the fire. The dogs slunk away so that he could hold out his hands to the flames. He would like to have turned and warmed his buttocks, but he had no wish to offend Sarah.

"He is up here," she said, and she opened the stair door and led him upstairs.

Unlike the kitchen, Tingle's chamber was chill and the smell was rank and sour with his sickness. There was one small brazier for heat and one candle standing in the window sill for light. Neither made a dint on the gloom of the winter afternoon. Sarah ushered James in and crossed to the bed where the man was lying.

"The scribe is here, grandfather," she murmured.

Tingle opened his eyes. "It took him long enough; a man could have shuffled off in half the time."

James went to apologize again, but with a wave of his hand Tingle stopped him. His voice was hoarse but still full of authority. "Never mind that now. We will waste time." Sarah took a cloth from a bowl beside the bed and went to wipe her grandfather's forehead. He stopped her.

"No. Later. I hath a task to do. Leave us."

She obeyed without demur.

"Bring the candle closer to the bed," said Tingle.

He did so and was shocked to see how the disease had wasted the old man's flesh. When James had seen him last, he was big and broad-shouldered. Now he was shrunken to half his former size, his head was skull-like and his hands skeletal. From beneath his sleeping hood, his white hair straggled lank about his face.

He groaned. "Give me the opiate." He motioned to the vial that was on a table next to the bed. James handed it to him, and helped him sit up so he could swallow. His mouth was thick with cancres and stank abominably.

"Enough. I have need of my wit." His eyes were yellowish and sunken but the look he fixed on the scribe was fierce. "No doubt you are full of wonderment as to the reason for this summons."

"Whatever is your wish, sire," said James, but his reply seemed to irritate the old man.

"Not too politic, Master Kennett. Too much politic rots the soul." He sank back, gasping. "How long has our Sovereign Lady, the Queen reigned?" he asked suddenly.

"Almost seventeen years, Master Tingle," replied James, puzzled at the question.

"The holy maid of Kent prophesied the king would die within a month of his marriage to Mistress Boleyn, but he didn't. He lived on another twelve years."

He coughed violently and spat into a bowl lying next to him. There was bright red blood in the sputum. James waited until he was calm again.

"I beg pardon, sire, is it another testament you wish me to write?"

"Nay. That is settled."

James was relieved. Tingle had made his will when he first acknowledged the wasting sickness had afflicted him. He had only one son and all his goods and chattels were left to him. There seemed no reason a dispute would arise.

"I heard him say it was the weeping time of the wretched world, but I do not believe that age was so very different. Men die at this queen's whim with as much pain. And some with as much courage."

James could see that Master Tingle, although clear in his wits, was burdened with too many thoughts for them to come out clearly. To his surprise the old man smiled, if you could call the grimace on the cadaverous face a smile.

"You want your story seamless and orderly, I can see, not tumbling out like pebbles in the spring thaw." He coughed again so harshly that James wondered if he was going to bring up his own bowels. "Very well. We can begin. But I hath breath for only one telling of my tale. You must write it down as I say it and not question me at every stop."

James placed his scribe's box on his knees and took out a sheaf of paper and some quills. He dipped one into the inkwell.

Tingle started. "This document is as told by Mr. Ned Tingle, who himself being unable to read nor write, has engaged the scribe, Master James Kennett, who is only recording what is said and not in any way complicitous with what is recounted."

The young scribe felt a twinge of fear. A disclaimer was all very well, but he had no fancy to be the ear to some traitorous secret.

Tingle continued. "I thought myself well favoured to be the King's servant. Steady wages, lodgings. I was married, two growing bairns, one suckling and another under the apron. I had found a position for my younger brother, Daniel, and he was taken on as a bridge-keeper."

He moaned quietly, reached for the opiate, changed his mind, and waited for the wave of pain to subside. Then he turned so he could see the scribe better. "Master Kennett, I put you this case. If the Antichrist himself appeared before you in this very room and said, 'Unless you swear to renounce all the teachings of God himself as we have received them, you will suffer a death so horrible it can hardly bear witness,' would you swear such an oath?"

The smoky candlelight was making pools of shadow on Tingle's face. Praying this was not a trap set by the devil who was now inhabiting the old man's body, James considered the question. "If I knew for certain it was the Antichrist, I would not so swear."

Tingle grinned his grin of a fiend. "Well said, my sprig. But what if I said that you would be hung by the neck until you were between two worlds, the quick and the dead. And that then you would be pulled back to life but only sufficient to know that your pizzle is cut off and stuffed in your mouth. And that if you were not yet dead, your innards are cut out and cast into a vat of boiling water. The stench from which is so vile, many who are witness, vomit. And finally, if you are still alive, your very heart is cut out and held before your eyes so it is the last thing you see on this earth." He caught

James by the sleeve of his doublet. "I put to you again: knowing full well this is the fate that will befall you, would you quail, and swear the oath even to the devil himself? And yeah undergo this suffering only for conscience sake?"

Mindful of Tingle's previous reprimand and also because he was an honest soul, James replied.

"Methinks I would so swear, sire. What are words but constructs of air here given out for another's connivance? My heart would know otherwise and I trust my Saviour would know the true thoughts of my heart and grant me forgiveness."

Tingle let go of James's arm. "A goodly answer. There were some few who did as you have so shrewdly posited. Then there were the hundreds of poor mortals such as myself, who did not give a jot what they would swear as long as they were not subject to these torments. However, the argument you have presented was used by his daughter, whom he dearly loved, and by his good wife. 'Take the oath in word only. Live for our sake.' But he refused their pleas and remained steadfast. Oh, this defiance was not because he was without imagination. Far from it. I had the night watch and when he was first imprisoned I oft heard him cry out in his sleep. When I was able, I would take him some small sustenance, bread sops or wine, for which he was most grateful. And he would hold discourse with me as if I were the keenest lawyer in the land."

He lay back on his pillow and James could see his chest heaving, his breath rasped. He was keeping himself alive by sheer effort of will.

"Once, I asked him why he, who had rejoiced at the burning of heretics, should see himself as so very different. Mr. Tyndale and Mr. Tunstall, after all, believed themselves to be right according to their conscience. He did not take offence but regarded me studiously. 'Tyndale was a heretic and an Antichrist, of that I am sure. But your point is taken.' And methinks it was, because in the last months he concerned himself much less with such things as had before inflamed him." Tingle sighed and waved his hand. "I have got away from my tale. Pray you write this down.

"I was one of the guards who helped him walk the way to his trial. I could see he thought even then he might be freed, as on a point of law, he had committed no malice. And he was a lawyer first and foremost. A monkish lawyer for sure but he was as adept as a dancing master at shifting and weaving. But we others knew he would be found guilty. Even without Mr. Rich's lies. The jury were too afraid for their own lives to acquit him and displease the king. He was frail by now, his beard grown long and unkempt. He wore a coarse woollen gown, and foolish wights, who think noblemen must perforce wear only velvet and ermine, did not know him. The whispers went through the crowd. Who is it? Who is it? I answered one fellow. It is Sir Thomas More, the one who was the King's chancellor." He paused. "I assume you know of him, master Kennett?"

"I have so, sir. He was an unrepentant Papist."

Tingle grimaced. "Methinks he would have been pleased with such an answer. He was never desirous of martyrdom. He wore a hair shirt all of his life, but secretly, so that no one would consider him like the Pharisee who wanted all the world to know of his righteousness."

"I see you much admired this Sir Thomas."

"I admired others equally as much. The priest John Fisher was nowhere near as comfortably off or as canny. He was a good old man and he should have died in his warm bed, surrounded by honour and love, not as he did, stripped naked before strangers and so thin his neck could have been severed with a kitchen knife. And the five monks of the Charterhouse, who died in the manner I have described. These I sore pitied and loved for their courage. They each could see what was happening to the one before and they did not renounce their belief."

He stopped, and James could see he was remembering and wished he could give him comfort. Then the withered hand was raised again, the signal to continue.

"On the return journey the procession was led by the executioner, his great axe with the blade pointed towards the prisoner so the crowd would know the verdict ..." Tingle smiled slightly. "I am aware it has been whispered in the village that I wore the red horns, but there is no truth in it. I was never the King's executioner, merely one of the guards at the Tower ... As we approached the prison gates, his son and his beloved daughter pushed through the throng of guards and halberdiers to say their final farewells. John More knelt for his father's blessing but Margaret clung to his neck, kissing him and weeping sorely." Another pause and a wag of the finger. Kennett stopped writing.

"I understand," said Tingle, "that his son-in-law, Roper, in relating these events, wrote that for many of those present, this sight was so lamentable that it made them also mourn and shed tears. It was true that Margaret's love and her sorrow filled the very air we were breathing and many did cry with her. But not all. Perhaps not near as many as Master Roper would have hoped for. What was it to them who laboured daily only to cover their own wretched bodies, to see such a one? The King and his court were the players, not they. And many more had long ago hardened their hearts to the suffering of other men. Various stories grew up after his death, as they always do. One was put out that on this day Sir Thomas More smelt as sweet and odoriferous as one of the saints. But I can tell you, there was nothing supernatural about it. I was present when the lieutenant of the Tower, Mr. Kingston, gave him some rose water and musk to perfume his clothes. Better than the stink of the Tower. The final story that has gone into the world concerns his head, but I will tell the truth of that in a moment. First give me some opiate. This biting in my stomach is fain to distract me completely."

James brought the vial to the old man's mouth.

"They had no such ointments or salves when the rack had finished with them. I count myself fortunate. But quickly, I am not done. Six days later, Sir Thomas More went to the scaffold. The King in his clemency declared he would die by the axe and not the true death of a traitor as Mr. Reynolds and the monks of the Charterhouse had so recently suffered. The time of the execution was set for nine of the clock in the morning. At mine own request, I was one of the guards attending him. Secretly, I offered to bring him wine or mandragora, but he refused. He was composed, walking to Tower Hill with his red cross in front of him. A wind coming up from the river ruffled his long beard. He was weak and needed to be helped climb the scaffold, making a joke about it which pleased those around. The King had requested that he not speak long so he did not. Why he obeyed I know not. Perhaps he was in a hurry now to go to the lap of God where he would be merry for eternity. Perhaps even then he feared his innards could be ripped from him if he gave offence. The executioner received his piece of gold and his blessing. He was after all merely the King's servant and not to be blamed. He did his task well and Sir Thomas' head fell into the basket on one clean stroke."

He ceased to talk and James saw that once again he was remembering. His eyes glistened with tears he refused to shed. Outside, the wind soughed through the black-barked trees and the snow pattered against the window pane. The brazier needed more wood but the scribe was afraid to interrupt the narrative which was now flowing so freely. He shifted his buttocks a little on the hard stool. Tingle raised his hand and James picked out a fresh quill.

"As was with all traitors, More's head was parboiled then stuck on a pike on top of London bridge for all to see and take heed. It had been there more than a seven night when the events I am about to relate took place.

"I had finished my watch for the night and returned to my lodgings at seven of the clock. The summer sun had not shown its face for many days and the morning proved drear, threatening rain. When I entered my chambers, I found my wife, Susanna, and my brother Daniel who lodged with us, were seated at the table. When she saw me, my wife flew into my arms.

"'Daniel will have us all burned as traitors and our children orphaned or burnt with us!'

"I calmed her until she could speak sensibly. Daniel meanwhile stared into the floor as if he could read his fate in the pattern of the rushes.

"'He has agreed Sir Thomas More's daughter can have the head from off the bridge. She has offered him four angels of gold if he will throw it to her. I beseech you, Ned, forbid him. 'Tis not only him will be blamed. We all will die or be racked to tell.'

"I had seen Margaret Roper and her father together when she visited him in his cell. He lay with his head in her lap while she soothed and stroked his brow as she was wont to do when they were at home. Now her father was named a traitor which he was not, and that same beloved face was soiled by birds and flies on top of London bridge. Eventually all of the heads were tossed into the river but only at his Majesty's command, never before or at anyone else's say so.

"'Is this true, brother?' I asked, although 'twas clear from Daniel's frightened face that it was.

"''Tis a little thing, Ned. I shall say the wind blew it off.'

"I rushed at him and fetched him such a cuff across his head, he almost fell from his chair.

"'Has this same wind ever blown off a head that is so rammed on a pike, it cannot be turned? Answer me! So long as you have been walking the bridge length, have you known the wind to lift off one of these heads? Answer!' Another hard slap that caused some flow of blood from his nose.

"'Brother, please, this is of concern to me alone. She will pay well.'

"I shoved him to the floor in disgust. 'You are worse than a fool. Will gold stop the rack from ripping your limbs from their sockets and shredding your flesh like cloth? It will not!'

"I caught him by the hair, jerking back his head. 'Will gold put out the flames when your hair catches fire as they burn you for a traitor? It will not!'

"He tried to roll away, crying. ''Tis not just the gold, Ned. She is a good woman.'

"I banged his head to the floor. 'Was not the maid of Kent a good woman? It did not save her. Nor Mr. Reynolds and the other monks. And were not they good men? And their death was horrible beyond imagining. You saw it.'

"My blood was running so hot I know not when I would have left off hurting him, but my wife caught me by the sleeve.

"'Enough, Ned.'

"My own bairns were wailing at her knees, and seeing them, I was sick in my heart. I stepped back and let Daniel get to his feet.

"'Susanna is right. When the constable comes looking he will blame all of us. And don't think it would be treated frivolously. The King will burn or hang anyone who sides against him. Especially with one such as Thomas More who defied him to the end. And this was a man he had loved and favoured. Do you think he gives a rush about a bridge keeper or his family? I will answer for you, Master Daniel. He does not! We are as but the parings of his toe nails.'

"Daniel wiped at his mouth. 'What shall I do? I have agreed. Mistress Roper will pass beneath the bridge at five of the clock today. I am to throw the head into the boat.'

"I turned away so as not to hit him again. Even in his whining, I did not trust him to be resolute.

"'I will take your watch. You must feign sickness. Nay, more, you must be made ill. Susanna, go at once and make up a purge. A strong one.' Daniel protested no more. Susanna hurried to do what I said and I went straightway to the bridge. On some few prior occasions, I had taken my brother's place when he was not able and it mattered not to the other guard. I took up the halberd and walked to the centre of the bridge. Crows flapped away at my approach. A welcome wind blew away the stench of the rotting heads. Sir Thomas' head, distinguished by the long beard, was to the centre, flanked by the heads of the five monks of the Charterhouse. I looked up at them all, still recognizable for the men they had been in spite of the birds, and I hoped it was true what Sir Thomas had believed. That they were all now together in heaven and making merry there.

"The hours crawled as I walked the watch. The air grew chillier and the river was flowing fast and dark. Finally, by the call of the watch, it was a quarter to the hour. Heavy drops of rain began to fall, pocking the river. I wondered if she would come. As slowly as I dared I once again marched to the centre of the bridge. And then I saw the boat coming fast down the river and I leaned over the wall. She saw me and stood up, keeping her balance in the bobbing boat by sheer wanting. They were within several yards of the bridge now and, pulling hard, the two oarsmen turned so that the bow was against the tide. They were strong men both but even so they could not hold much longer and the boat began to slip. She called something to me but the wind seized her words and I could not hear. It was apparent what she had said, however, and I shook my head, making it plain that I would not fulfill her request. She lifted up a pouch, holding it to me pleadingly. One of the boatsmen shouted. They could not hold much longer. The boat was being turned around. I waved my arms indicating she must move away. In a moment, she would have been gone and I would have returned to the safety of my lodgings. But she dropped the pouch of money and the hood of the dark monkish cloak she was wearing for secrecy fell back. The pelting rain was soaking her hair and streaking her face. She raised her hands, palms upwards, beseechingly.

"Then, as if without my own will, my mouth opened and a cry burst forth that I have never uttered before or since. I cannot say whence came such a sound but it seized hold of my very flesh as if the wailing and my body were one and the same. I jumped up on the railing, seized the head from off the pike and with yet another shout, 'Take it!,' I tossed it from the bridge. There was a basket filled with straw in the bow and the head landed there ... The last sight I had was of Margaret Roper reaching forward to touch the beloved face she had caressed so often before. Then the boatsmen dipped their oars and they shot away on the racing tide."

Tingle had been speaking so quickly that James had difficulty keeping up and his fingers were cramping on the quill, but here the old man stopped.

"Were you punished, sire?" James asked.

"Verily. I was put in the pillory. Wishing to demonstrate their loyalty to the King, my fellow guards were strong in their revilement of me. I was pelted with their filth and the filth of the dogs of the street for three days. Sir Thomas' daughter too was imprisoned but soon released. She gave nothing away and said that her prayers had been answered, no doubt by an angel of God, and that is why the head had fallen into her boat. Later that is the story that some people believed. Others said it was indeed angels that caused the head to jump, but they were of solid gold. All were wrong."

"Did she not make good her promise?"

"Ay, she did. As soon as it was safe to do so, she sent money. Queen Anne's execution followed hard on that of Sir Thomas, and soon after I left the King's service and came here to this village. In the years that have followed, God has seen fit both to give and to take away. I have lost my wife and two bairns but I have prospered."

He fought back another spate of coughing, which seemed to exhaust him more than ever. James waited patiently, sensing the story was not yet complete. Tingle raised his hand and pointed.

"See that cupboard by the window? Put down your box and go to it."

James obeyed.

"Open the drawer as far as it will go and feel with your hand behind it … Good. There is a strip of wood, turn it widdershins and pull down gently."

James did so and felt the circlet of wood come loose in his hand.

"In that hole, you will find a pouch. Have you got it?"

"Yes, sire."

"Bring it here."

James took the pouch, which was of soft leather. He placed it on the bed. With shaking hands, Tingle loosened the thong at the neck and upturned it on the coverlet. Out slipped four gold coins. James could see the stamp of his Majesty, King Henry.

"This was my payment. As you see I have not touched it. There were many times when I was sorely tempted. When my own children were in want. But I did not do so."

Leaving the coins where they lay, he indicated to James to take up his quill.

"I leave this money herewith to one Master James Kennett, scribe, in payment for his services."

James gasped. "But sire, that is one hundred times more than the fee."

"I am aware of that. And shortly I will call in witnesses to see that I am in sound mind and that you have not stolen the money. You are a goodly young fellow, Master Kennett. I have known you from a child. With this money you can go to London and study the law as I have heard you have dreamed of doing."

His voice was now so low and hoarse he was almost inaudible.

"Fret not, Master scribe. This is not a whim, it is my long considered desire. Now, I wish you to read through this account of mine as I have told it."

"Is there, is there any particular thing you would fain I do with the story, sire, after …"

"After I die? No. You can keep it or not as you wish, or as my son wishes, although he will not be happy for the giving of the money.

A curate has shriven me, so I do not go to my death with my sins weighing on my soul as some men do. I could see by your look when you came that you expected I would have guilt to assuage. But my story is not of that." He breathed as deeply as he could. "On the bridge that afternoon, I saw no winged angel, nothing that I, a worldly man, would ascribe to God's manifestation. But since that day, I have held to my bosom a sliver of belief, fragile as icicles, that for one moment I was God's servant; and that for one short, precious moment, I stayed the tears of the weeping world."

He tapped the coverlet. "Now, Mr. Kennett, please read back to me my tale. I would fain gaze into its glass and be merry therein."

Catamount

by

RUTH RENDELL

THE SKY WAS the biggest she had ever seen. They said the skies of Suffolk were big and the skies of Holland, but those were small, cozy, by comparison. It might belong on another planet, covering another world. Mostly a pale soft azure or a dark hard blue, it was sometimes overcast with huge rolling cumulus, swollen and edged with sharp white light, from which rain roared without warning.

Chuck and Carrie's house was only the second built up there, under that sky. The other was what they called a modular home and Nora a prefab, a frame bungalow standing on a bluff between the dirt road and the ridge. The Johanssons who lived there kept a few cows and fattened white turkeys for Thanksgiving. It was—thank God, said Carrie—invisible from her handsome log house, built of yellow Montana pine. She and Chuck called it Elk Valley Ranch, a name

Nora had thought pretentious when she read it on their headed notepaper but not when she saw it. The purpose of the letter was to ask her and Gordon to stay and she could hardly believe it, it seemed too glorious, the idea of a holiday in the Rocky Mountains, though she and Carrie had been best friends for years. That was before she married a captain in the U.S. Air Force stationed at Bentwaters and went back home to Colorado with him.

It was August when they went the first time. The little plane from Denver took them to the airport at Hogan and Carrie met them in the Land Cruiser. The road ran straight and long, parallel with the Crystal River that was also straight, like a canal, with willows and cottonwood trees along its banks. Beyond the flat flowery fields the mountains rose, clothed in pine and scrub oak and aspen, mountains that were dark, almost black, but with green sunlit meadows bright between the trees. The sun shone and it was hot but the sky looked like a winter sky in England, the blue very pale and the clouds stretched across it like torn strips of chiffon.

There were a few small houses, many large barns and stables. Horses were in the fields, one chestnut mare with a new-born foal. Carrie turned in towards the western mountains and through a gateway with ELK VALLEY RANCH carved on a board. It was still a long way to the house. The road wound through curves and hairpin bends and as they went higher the mountain slopes and the green canyons opened out below them, mountain upon mountain and valley upon valley, a herd of deer in one deep hollow, a golden eagle perched on a spar. By the roadside grew yellow asters and blue Michaelmas daisies, wild delphiniums, pale pink geraniums and the bright red Indian paintbrush, and above the flowers brown and yellow butterflies hovered.

"There are snakes," Carrie said. "Rattlesnakes. You have to be a bit careful. One of them was on the road last night. We stopped to look at it and it lashed against our tires."

"I'd like to see a porcupine." Gordon had his Rocky Mountains wildlife book with him, open on his knees. "But I'd settle for a raccoon."

"You'll very likely see both," Carrie said. "Look, there's the house."

It stood on the crown of a wooded hill, its log walls a dark gamboge, its roof green. A sheepdog came down to the five-barred gate when it saw the Land Cruiser.

"You must have spectacular views," Gordon said.

"We do. If you wake up early enough you see fabulous things from your window. Last week I saw the cougar."

"What's a cougar?"

"Mountain lion. I'll just get out and open the gate."

It wasn't until she was home again in England that Nora had looked up the cougar in a Mammals of North America book. That night and for the rest of the fortnight she had forgotten it. There were so many things to do and see. Walking and climbing in the mountains, fishing in the Crystal River, picking a single specimen of each flower and pressing it in the book she bought for the purpose, photographing hawks and eagles, watching the chipmunks run along the fences. Driving down to the little town of Hogan, where on their way to Telluride, Butch Cassidy and Sundance had stopped to rob the bank, visiting the hotel where the Clanton Gang had left bullets from their handguns in the bathroom wall, shopping, sitting in the hot springs and swimming in the cold pool. Eating in Hogan's restaurant where elk steaks and rattlesnake burgers were specialties, and drinking in the Last Frontier Bar.

Carrie and Chuck said to come back next year or come in the winter when the skiing began. That was at the time when Hogan Springs was emerging as a ski resort. Or come in the spring when the snows melted and the alpine meadows burst into bloom, miraculous with gentians and avalanche lilies. And they did go again, but in late summer, a little later than in the previous year. The aspen leaves were yellowing, the scrub oak turning bronze.

"We shall have snow in a month," Carrie said.

A black bear had come with her cubs and eaten Lily Johansson's turkeys. "Like a fox at home," Gordon said. They went up to the top of Mount Opie in the new ski lift and walked down. It was five miles through fields of blue flax and orange gaillardias. The golden ridge and the pine-covered slopes looked serene in the early autumn sunshine, the skies were clear until late afternoon when the clouds gathered and the rain came. The rain was torrential for ten minutes and then it was hot and sunny again, the grass and wild flowers steaming. A herd of elk came close up to the house and one of them pressed its huge head and stubby horns against the window. They saw the black bear and her cubs through Chuck's binoculars, loping along down in the green canyon.

"One day I'll see the cougar," Nora said, and Gordon asked if cougars were an endangered species.

"I wouldn't think so. There are supposed to be mountain lions in every state of the United States, but I guess most of them are here. You ought to talk to Lily Johansson, she's often seen them."

"There was a boy got killed by one last fall," Carrie said. "He was cycling and the thing came out of the woods, pulled him off his bike and well—ate him, I suppose. Or started to eat him. It was scared off. They're protected, so there was nothing to be done."

Cougar stories abounded. Everyone had one. Some of them sounded like urban—rural, rather—myths. There was the one about the woman out walking with her little boy in Winter Park and who came face to face with a cougar on the mountain. She put the child on her shoulders and told him to hold up his arms so that, combined, they made a creature eight feet tall, which was enough to frighten the animal off. The boy in the harness shop in Hogan had one about the man out with his dog. To save himself he had to let the cougar kill and eat his dog while he got away. In the town Nora bought a reproduction of Audubon's drawing of a cougar, graceful, powerful, tawny, with a cat's mysterious closed-in face.

"I thought they were small, like a lynx," Gordon said.

"They're the size of an African lion—well, lioness. That's what they look like, a lioness."

"I shall frame my picture," Nora said, "and one day I'll see the real thing."

They came back to Hogan year after year. More houses were built but not enough to spoil the place. Once they came in winter but, at their age, it was too late to learn to ski. Seventeen feet of snow fell. The snow plough came out onto the roads on Christmas Eve and cleared a passage for cars, making ramparts of snow where the flowers had been. Nora wondered about the animals. What did they live on, these creatures? The deer ate the bark of trees. Chuck put cattle feed out for them and hay.

"The herds have been reduced enough by mountain lions," he said. "You once asked if they were endangered. There are tens of thousands of them now, more than there have ever been."

Nora worried about the golden eagle. What could it find to feed on in this white world? The bears were hibernating. Were the cougars also? No one seemed to know. She would never come again in winter when everything was covered, sleeping, waiting, buried. It was one thing for the skiers, another for a woman, elderly now, afraid to go out lest she slip on the ice. The few small children they saw had coloured balloons tied to them on long strings so that their parents could see and rescue them if they sank too deep down in the snow. All Christmas Day the sun blazed, melting the snow on the roof, and by night frost held the place in its grip, so that the guttering round the house grew a fringe of icicles.

The following spring Gordon died. Lily Johansson wrote a letter of sympathy, and when Jim Johansson died next Christmas Nora wrote one to her. She delayed going back to the mountains for a year, two years. Driving from the airport with Carrie, she noticed for the first time something strange. It was a beautiful landscape but not a comfortable one, not easeful, not conducive to peace and tranquility. There was no lushness and, even in the heat, no warmth. Lying in bed at night or sitting in a chair at dawn, watching for elk or the cougar, she tried to discover what was not so much wrong, it was far from wrong, but what made this feeling. The answer came to her uncompromisingly. It was fear. The countryside was full of fear, and the fear, while it added to the grandeur and in a strange way to the beauty, denied peace to the observer. Danger informed it, it threatened while it smiled. Always something lay in wait for you round the corner, though it might be only a beautiful butterfly. It never slept, it never rested even under snow. It was alive.

Lily Johansson came round for coffee. She was a large heavy woman with calloused hands who had had a hard life. Six children had been born to her, two husbands had died. She was alone, struggling to make a living from hiring out horses, from a dozen cows and turkeys. Every morning she got up at dawn, not because she had so much to do but because she couldn't sleep after dawn. The cougar, passing the night high up in the mountains, came down many mornings past Lily's fence to hunt along the green valley. It might be days before she came back to her mountain hide-out but she would come back, and next morning lope down the rocky path between the asters and the Indian paintbrush past Lily's fence.

"Why do you call it 'she'?" Nora asked. Was this an unlikely statement of feminist principles?

Lily smiled. "I guess on account of knowing she's a mother. There was weeks went by when I never saw her, and then one morning she comes down the trail and she's two young ones with her. Real pretty kittens they was."

"Do you ever speak to her?"

"Me? I'm scared of her. She'd kill me as soon as look at me. Sometimes I says to her, 'Catamount, catamount,' but she don't pay me no attention. You want to see her, you come down and stop over and maybe we'll see her in the morning."

Nora went a week later. They sat together in the evening, the two old widows, drinking Lily's root beer and talking of their dead husbands. Nora slept in a tiny bedroom, with linen sheets on the narrow bed and a picture on the wall of (appropriately) Daniel in the Lion's den. At dawn Lily came in with a mug of tea and told her to get up, put on her "robe" and they'd watch.

The eastern sky was black with stripes of red between the mountains. The hidden sun had coloured the snow on the peaks rosy pink. All the land lay still. Along the path where the cougar passed the flowers were still closed up for the night.

"What makes her come?" Nora whispered. "Does she see the dawn or feel it? What makes her get up from her bed and stretch and maybe wash her paws and her face and set off?"

"Are you asking me? I don't know. Who does? It's a mystery."

"I wish we knew."

"Catamount, catamount," said Lily. "Come, come, catamount."

But the cougar didn't come. The sun rose, a magnificent spectacle, almost enough to bring tears to your eyes, Nora thought, all that purple and rose and orange and gold, all those miles and miles of serene blue. She had coffee and bread and blueberry jam with Lily and then she went back to Elk Valley Ranch.

"One day I'll see her," she said to herself as she stroked the sheepdog and went to let herself in by the yard door.

But would she? She had almost made up her mind not to come back next year. This was young people's country and she was getting too old for it. It was for climbers and skiers and mountain bikers, it was for those who could withstand the cold and enjoy the heat.

Sometimes when she stood in the sun, its power frightened her, it was too strong for human beings. When rain fell it was a wall of water, a cascade, a torrent, and it might drown her. Snakes lay curled up in the long grass and spiders were poisonous. If anything could be too beautiful for human beings to bear, this was. Looking at it for long made her heart ache, filled her with strange undefined longings. At home once more in the mild and gentle English countryside, she looked at her Audubon and thought how this drawing of the cougar symbolized for her all that landscape, all that vast green and gold space, yet she had never seen it in the flesh, the bones, the sleek tawny skin.

Two years passed before she went back. It would be the last time. Chuck was ill and Elk Valley was no place for an old sick man. He and Carrie were moving to an apartment in Denver. They no longer walked in the hills or skied on the slopes or ate barbecue on the bluff behind the house. Chuck's heart was bad and Carrie had arthritis. Nora, who had always slept soundly at Elk Valley Ranch, now found that sleep eluded her; she lay awake for hours with the curtains drawn back, gazing at the black velvet starry sky and listening to the baying of the coyotes at the mountain's foot. Sleepless, she began getting up earlier and earlier and on the second morning, tip-toeing to the kitchen, she found that Carrie got up early too. They sat together, drinking coffee and watching the dawn.

The night of the storm she slept and awoke and slept till the thunder woke her at four. The storm was like nothing she had ever known, and she who had never been frightened by thunder and lightning was afraid now. The lightning lit the room with searchlight brilliance and while it lingered, dimming and brightening, for a moment too bright to look at, the thunder rolled and cracked as if the mountains themselves moved and split. Into the ensuing silence, the rain broke. If you were out in it, you couldn't defend yourself against it, it would beat you to the ground.

Carrie's calling fetched her out of her room. No lights were on. Carrie was feeling her way about in the dark.

"What is it?"

"Chuck's sick," Carrie said. "I mean, very sick. He's lying in bed on his back with his mouth all drawn down to one side and when he speaks his voice isn't like his voice, it's slurred, he can't form the words."

"How do you phone the emergency services? I'll do it."

"Nora, you can't. I've tried calling them. The phone's down. Why do you think I've no lights on? The power's gone."

"What shall we do? I don't suppose you want to leave him but I could do something."

"Not in this rain," Carrie said. "When it stops, could you take the Land Cruiser and drive into Hogan?"

Then Nora had to admit she had never learned to drive. They both went to look at Chuck. He seemed to be asleep, breathing noisily through his crooked mouth. A crash from somewhere overhead drove the women into each other's arms, to cling together.

"I'm going to make coffee," Carrie said.

They drank it, sitting near the window, watching the lightning recede, leap into the mountains. Nora said, "The rain's stopping. Look at the sky."

The black clouds were streaming apart to show the dawn. A pale tender sky, neither blue nor pink but halfway between, revealed itself as the banks of cumulus and the streaks of cirrus poured away over the mountain peak into the east. The rain lifted like a blind rolled up. One moment it was a cascade, the next it was gone, and the coming light showed gleaming pools of water and grass that glittered and sparkled.

"Try the phone again," Nora said.

"It's dead," said Carrie, and realizing what she'd said, shivered.

"Do you think Lily's phone would be working? I could go down there and see. If her phone's down too, maybe she'd drive me into Hogan."

"Please, Nora, would you? I can't leave him."

The air was so fresh, it made her dizzy. It made her think how seldom most people ever breathe such air as this or know what it is, but that once the whole world's atmosphere was like this, as pure and as clean. The sun was rising, a red ball in a sea of pale lilac, and while on the jagged horizon black clouds still massed, the huge deep bowl of sky was scattered over with pink and golden cirrus feathers. Soon the sun would be hot and the land and air as dry as a desert.

She made her way down the hairpin bends of the mountain road, aware of how poor a walker she had become. An ache spread from her thighs into her hips, particularly on the right side, so that in order to make any progress she was forced to limp, shifting her weight onto the left. But she was near Lily Johansson's house now. Lily's two horses stood placidly by the gate into the field.

Then, suddenly, they wheeled round and cantered away down the meadow as if the sight of her had frightened them. She said aloud, "What's wrong? What's happened?"

As if in answer the animal came out of the flowery path onto the surface of the road. She was the size of an African lioness, so splendidly loose-limbed and in control of her long fluid body that she seemed to flow from the grass and the asters and the pink geraniums. On the road she stopped and turned her head. Nora could see her amber eyes and the faint quiver of her golden cheeks. She forgot about making herself tall, putting her hands high above her head, advancing menacingly. She was powerless, gripped by the beauty of this creature, this cougar she had longed for. And she was terribly afraid.

"Catamount, catamount," she whispered but no voice came.

The cougar dropped onto her belly, a quivering cat flexing her muscles, as she prepared to spring.

Clay Pillows

by

JAMES POWELL

THE TINY CHURCH had four lancet windows and a crowded Stations-of-the-Cross. At the end of the funeral mass the priest left the altar to shake the smoking censer and holy water over Uncle Clarence's coffin. Then he disappeared into the sacristy through a lancet-shaped doorway.

Tom O'Malley, a balding, tired-faced man in his sixties, knelt to say a final prayer for his uncle and found himself saying another for Mr. Gregory, the man O'Malley had shot and killed so many years before. Had all the church ceremony brought Mr. Gregory and his bare-bones burial to mind? Uncle Clarence said he'd dug a hole in the ground in the woods behind the farmhouse and tumbled the body in. He would never show O'Malley where. "Don't dwell on it, Tommy. Self-defence cut and dried."

The farm was on the edge of town. O'Malley recognized the man limping quickly up the dirt road from his uncle's description. When Mr. Gregory came bursting through the door waving a revolver O'Malley, who'd never held a firearm before in all his eighteen years, had found the pistol and was holding it out at arm's length using both hands to keep it steady. The intruder fired first. O'Malley shot back. Mr. Gregory clutched his chest and fell to the floor with blood spilling from his mouth.

In the next moment Uncle Clarence was standing in the doorway breathing hard. He knelt down by the body. "Dead," he said, shaking his head. "I saw him get off the bus. He didn't see me. Don't know how he found us. But he set off this way like a man who knew where he was going. I followed close as I could."

Astonished by what he'd done, O'Malley stood frozen to the spot.

"I'll take it from here, Tommy," said Uncle Clarence, grabbing the body under the armpits and dragging it toward the door. Seeing the smear of blood on the linoleum O'Malley went to be sick.

O'MALLEY SAT BACK, alone in the front pew reserved for family. Mike, his older brother by a year, wasn't there. Nor were any of his sisters, though Uncle Clarence had provided for them all and taken care of their mother, his older and favourite sister, until she died ten years ago.

He turned in the pew. Beyond the opened doors of the church the undertaker's men were butting their cigarettes before coming inside to deal with the coffin.

Now O'Malley examined the mourners. Half a van-load had come from St. Mary's Village, the retirement home where his uncle had lived since his recent stroke. The others were a few of Victory Public Relations' older clients.

In 1944 with the end of the war in sight many Toronto businesses starting up were calling themselves Victory this or Victory that. As a young boy O'Malley didn't know what public relations was. But he suspected it had to do with the shady side of the street where his father did his walking.

O'Malley followed the coffin out into the bright June day. The warm breeze promised summer but still carried a chill edge to it. The retirement home people couldn't go to the gravesite because their van had been scheduled for a trip to the shopping mall in Humber. But the other mourners got in their cars and fell in behind the hearse and limousine as the funeral procession set off at the measured pace of rented solemnity, passing through the old part of town where roots of the large trees shouldered the sidewalk pavement about and English daisies spotted the lawns.

O'Malley rode in the limousine with the priest, now in white surplice and black stole, who mentioned visiting the deceased at St. Mary's and how he found him a kindred spirit. O'Malley gave the man a long glance before remembering his mother had said that after getting out of the army Uncle Clarence had given serious thought to going into the seminary. The priest went on to describe the stained glass half-window the deceased had willed the church, a pelican feeding its young with its own blood, which would go between the last two Stations of the Cross.

O'Malley's mind was elsewhere. He was remembering his great surprise when Uncle Clarence stepped in "to hold the fort," as he put it, after O'Malley's father's second heart attack. There was nothing shady-side-of-the-street about his uncle. The man's upright air was helped along by the tailored three-piece navy blue suit and grey fedora he'd bought with his army gratuity money. In fact his decision to stay on after O'Malley's father got back on his feet made young O'Malley wonder if he'd been wrong about the family business.

After O'Malley Senior died Uncle Clarence took over, closed down the office and moved Victory Public Relations out of town. But he visited them every month, coming after nightfall. Answer the door and there he'd be with a prepared smile. He and O'Malley's mother would sit at the table in the dining alcove and he would go over the bills and write out the cheques. Then they would talk in low voices for a while. On his way out Uncle Clarence always stopped to speak to O'Malley's brother Mike who, it was understood, would go into the family business when he got out of high school. Then Uncle Clarence would give the rest of them a quick look as if making sure they were all there.

THE CEMETERY WAS out past the fair grounds. The slow drive through the countryside reminded O'Malley of the morning train out of Union Station which they took each August to Duck Lake, one of the Muskoka region's archipelago of lakes. When they got off the train Uncle Clarence would be there to drive them to a rented cottage where they learned to swim and handle the rowboat. His uncle's only concession to summer was a Panama hat and, once or twice if the day was very hot, he would take off his shoes and socks and sit on the dock dangling white feet in the water.

The summer at the cottage after Mike graduated from high school he and Uncle Clarence started taking long walks in the woods around the lake. That summer ended with Mike's sudden announcement that he would enter the seminary that fall. At the time O'Malley thought that's what they'd been talking about on those walks, Mike's priestly vocation. Who, least of all Uncle Clarence, could object to having a priest in the family? Suddenly O'Malley became the one destined for Victory Public Relations.

AT EASTER VACATION the following year his uncle took O'Malley along on a business trip to Niagara Falls, using the drive to give the boy a fuller explanation of what Victory Public Relations did. "Some people want to keep their names before the public eye," he said. "Say anything about them good or bad as long as you mention their name. That's the city side of things. Then there's our side, the small town side, people who'd be just as happy if they didn't get talked about at all."

And he explained how O'Malley's father got into the business. "He and a Mr. Gregory made a modest score in a penny mining stock swindle. Your father was holding the money. On his way to divvy up Mr. Gregory, a bit in his celebratory cups, drove into a tree. While his partner was in the hospital your father, whose bum ticker needed less strenuous work, decided to do the disappearing act with the ill-gotten gains. He used the money to buy out another gentleman who proved to be the better swindler, grossly exaggerating the value of the dark secrets in his possession."

"You're saying we're blackmailers?" asked the boy, more disappointed than surprised.

Uncle Clarence, who seldom took his eyes off the road, looked over at him. "Tommy, we have to play the hand we're dealt. The money may be slow but it's steady. Remember, we have your sisters and your mother to take care of. Thank the Lord for the small town sense of shame."

Niagara Falls was a place of mists, booming water and rainbows. The high-end buyers used a large hotel downtown. Uncle Clarence stayed at a small, damp motel closer to the falls. The sellers who came there were peddling the bottom scrapings of their barrels. He heard them out and if he bought he paid them from small sums of money he'd hidden about the motel room.

Not long after the Niagara trip O'Malley's brother Mike left the seminary and moved to Vancouver to look for work. The priesthood had been his way of avoiding the family business.

When O'Malley made noises about finding another line of work, too, Uncle Clarence urged him to give things a chance. "I wasn't that happy at first myself," he admitted. "Here's some advice your father gave me. Oh, he had a rather deep bag of tricks behind the Irish good looks, your father. 'Tell them you're only the hired help,' he said. 'Make them believe a Mr. Gregory runs the operation.' That's right, using the name of the partner he'd swindled was your father's idea of a joke. 'Make Mr. Gregory a hard-hearted son-of-a-gun,' he said. 'Commiserate with them. Say you're sorry but Mr. Gregory has to have more money.' Well, he hit the nail on the head. It does make it easier.

"And speaking of Mr. Gregory, your father thought he could sit back in an office with Victory Public Relations on the door and watch the money roll in. But right after I came on board he saw his old partner limping down a nearby street. Just in case Mr. Gregory had tracked him down your father gave me his pistol to keep in my desk in the outer office. Sure enough one day when I was there alone Mr. Gregory burst in mad as hell waving a gun and pushed by me into your father's office. I got out the pistol and sent him off dragging a wing and swearing he'd get even. So if you ever see a tall guy with a limp and a shock of ginger hair you'd be wise to do the same. I'll show you where I keep the pistol."

To sweeten the pot Uncle Clarence promised to teach O'Malley how to drive. He himself had come to driving late in life and didn't really enjoy it. And there was a lot of driving. "We make our collections personally," he explained. "We aren't in the line of work where we give out our address."

O'Malley remembered visiting their first client, a Mrs. Sutwell whose dark secret he never discovered. "You stay here," said Uncle Clarence. "I should have warned you to bring a book." He was gone for several hours. When he came back he said, "A very lonely woman and one great talker."

When the woman died a few years back she left Uncle Clarence money in her will. "Ah, there are going to be a lot of tin ears in heaven," he said.

THE FUNERAL PROCESSION drove between the two brick columns into the cemetery parking area. The Catholic corner was set apart by stanchions and a chain. An undertaker's man opened a section of the chain and the hearse moved inside.

By the time the mourners made the walk from the parking lot to the cemetery plot the coffin lay over the open grave on the broad straps of the mechanism to lower it into the ground. Everyone gathered around on carpets of artificial grass laid over the raw earth.

When O'Malley's uncle had his stroke he had written everyone telling them Mr. Gregory had died, taking their secrets with him to the grave, and that Victory Public Relations was no more. Even so these few had come to bid Uncle Clarence goodbye.

There were the Dixons, she in her furs and he in his dove grey chauffeur's uniform. When Dixon deserted his unit in World War II she spread the story that he'd been killed in action. He returned home with a beard and they pretended he was her chauffeur who lived in a room over the garage.

There were the Peacocks. When the first Mr. Peacock died he left her a substantial yearly income provided she never remarried. Later she fell in love with a man who was as reluctant as she was to give up the money. So instead, he changed his name to Peacock and moved in.

Next to them was Dora Burke of the Burke sisters looking her age at last. Her older sister Maude liked to dress up in the youngest fashions. Dora preferred an older, more conservative wardrobe. Their reputation for eccentric dress concealed the fact that they were unwed mother and daughter.

At the grave's edge was George Farley looking very sad for he had faced Uncle Clarence across the cribbage board for years. Farley was a client by inheritance, so to speak. An elderly relative he knew only slightly had invited Farley to come for a visit, promising the trip would be to his profit. His host lived in a substantial yellow brick house in a town whose wide main street declared that it served a farm community where horses and wagons had once been common. One night the relative took Farley up to the attic and unlocked a door to a small room. There in a chair with her wrists between her knees sat a middle-aged woman with a round face and vacant eyes humming to herself. The man spoke to her kindly and called her Cousin Gladys. The tuneless humming continued. Farley's relative closed the door. As he turned the key in the lock he cautioned, "Watch out for her. Our Cousin Gladys is a crafty one."

On the way downstairs he told Farley that when he died his estate would go to Farley if he promised to take care of Cousin Gladys until she died and keep her existence a secret from everyone. He also mentioned the encumbrance of the blackmail payments, the result of a disgruntled housekeeper let go when his wife was still alive.

On O'Malley's first visit to the Farleys he and his uncle stayed for dinner during which Farley passed over an envelope. "Here's for Mr. Gregory."

"Mr. Gregory thanks you," said Uncle Clarence.

Afterwards, while Mrs. Farley was clearing away the dishes so her husband and Uncle Clarence could play some cribbage, O'Malley said he thought he heard the front door close. Farley jumped up. "Cousin Gladys is out again," he said.

Farley drove them down quiet streets of houses whose living rooms were lit a dim blue from early television screens. All of them squinted into the rain and darkness. "We've got to find her before she catches her death of cold," said Mrs. Farley.

Farley took them to places Cousin Gladys had gone before, a culvert under the railroad tracks, a tree-house behind an empty Queen Anne, an old tool shed. Finally he parked the car in front of the town band shell next to the heavy old machine-gun, a memorial to the World War I dead. Farley got out, removed a section of lattice-work around the base of the band shell and ducked inside. A moment later he came out with his arm around Cousin Gladys, humming to herself as best she could through lips trembling with cold. When they got back to the house Mrs. Farley took her up for a hot bath.

Years later Cousin Gladys died. While Farley and Uncle Clarence played cribbage upstairs O'Malley dug a hole in the dirt floor in the basement and buried her. When he was done they gathered for prayers over the body. "We will all of us lay down our heads on clay pillows soon enough," Uncle Clarence said.

Now the thing in the attic became the hump of dirt in the basement. The Farleys continued their payments.

AT THE END of the graveside ceremony the other mourners drifted back to the parking lot. O'Malley remained a little longer. It was hard for him to let go of something he'd been trying to figure out all these years. Oh, he knew why he'd stayed in the blackmailing business. On good days he'd say he owed it to his uncle who'd helped him dispose of Mr. Gregory's body. On bad days it was because his uncle knew where that body was buried. But why had Uncle Clarence stayed?

O'Malley shook his head. Well, the priest and the limousine were waiting. As he turned his back on the grave he saw a tall, grey-headed man limping quickly toward him. He recognized Mr. Gregory, the man he'd shot over forty years ago. Mr. Gregory passed O'Malley with a muttered "I'm sorry I'm late. I expect I'll be late for my own funeral" and went to stand at the grave's edge in silence before adding his handful of earth to the coffin's lid.

When he turned and saw O'Malley's face he smiled. "No, I'm not a violation of the one-dead-man-per-funeral rule," he said. "I thought Clarence would have told you by now. No matter. My name's George Musgrove. Your uncle and I were good friends in the war. He saved my life when I got this." He slapped his leg. "I was only trying to help him out. He said he needed you. That little charade of ours, he said that was something he'd learned from your father who had, I remember him putting it, a rather deep bag of tricks."

On *The Anatomisation of an Unknown Man* (1637) by Frans Mier

by

JOHN CONNOLLY

I

The painting titled *The Anatomisation of an Unknown Man* is one of the more obscure works by the minor Dutch painter, Frans Mier. It is an unusual piece, although its subject matter may be said to be typical of our time: the opening up of a body by what is, one initially assumes, a surgeon or anatomist, the light from a suspended lamp falling over the naked body of the anonymous man, his scalp peeled back to reveal his skull, his innards exposed as the anatomist's blade hangs suspended above him, ready to explore further the intricacies of his workings, the central physical component of the universe's rich complexity.

I was not long ago in England, and witnessed there the hanging of one Elizabeth Evans—Canberry Bess, they called her—a notorious murderer and cutpurse, who was taken with her partner, one Thomas Shearwood. Counterey Tom was hanged and then gibbeted at Gray's Inn fields, but it was the fate of Elizabeth Evans to be dissected after her death at the Barber-Surgeons' Hall, for the body of a woman is of more interest to the surgeons than the body of a man, and harder to come by. She wept and screamed as she was brought to the gallows, and cried out for a Christian burial, for the terror of the Hall was greater to her than that of the noose itself. Eventually, the hangman silenced her with a rag, for she was disturbing the crowd.

Something of her fear had communicated itself to the onlookers, though, for there was a commotion at the gallows, as I recall. Although the surgeons wore the guise of commoners, yet the crowd knew them for what they were, and a shout arose that the woman had suffered enough under the Law, and that she should have no further barbarities visited upon her, although I fear their concern was less for the dignity of her repose than the knowledge that the mob was to be deprived of the display of her carcass in chains at St. Pancras, and the slow exposure of her bones at King's Cross. Still, the surgeons had their way for, when the hangman was done with her, she was cut down and stripped of her apparel, then laid naked in a chest and thrown into a cart. From there, she was carried to the Hall near unto Cripplegate. For a penny, I was permitted, with others, to watch as the surgeons went about their work, and a revelation it was to me.

But I digress. I merely speak of it to stress that Mier's painting cannot be understood in isolation. It is a record of our time, and should be seen in the context of the work of Valverde and Estienne, of Spigelius and Berrettini and Berengarius, those other great illustrators of the inner mysteries of our corporeal form.

Yet look closer and it becomes clear that the subject of Mier's paint-ing is not as it first appears. The unknown man's face is contorted in its final agony, but there is no visible sign of strangulation, and his neck is unmarked. If he is a malefactor taken from the gallows, then by what means was his life ended? Although the light is dim, it is clear that his hands have been tied to the anatomist's table by means of stout rope. Only the right hand is visible, admittedly, but one would hardly secure one and not the other. On his wrist are gashes where he has struggled against his bonds, and blood pours from the table to the floor in great quantities. The dead do not bleed in this way.

And if this is truly a surgeon, then why does he not wear the attire of a learned man? Why does he labour alone in some dank place, and not in a hall or theatre? Where are his peers? Why are there no other men of science, no assistants, no curious onlookers enjoying their penny's worth? This, it would appear, is secret work.

Look: there, in the corner, behind the anatomist, head tilted to stare down at the dissected man. Is that not the head and upper body of a woman? Her left hand is raised to her mouth, and her eyes are wide with grief and horror, but here too a rope is visible. She is also restrained, although not so firmly as the anatomist's victim. Yes, perhaps "victim" is the word, for the only conclusion to be drawn is that the man on the table has suffered under the knife. This is no corpse from the gallows, and this is not a dissection.

This is something much worse.

II

The question of attribution is always difficult in such circumstances. It resembles, one supposes, the investigation into the commission of a crime. There are clues left behind by the murderer, and it is the work of an astute and careful observer to connect such evidence to the man responsible. The use of a single source of light, shining from right to left, is typical of Mier. So, too, is the elongation of the faces, so that they resemble wraiths more than people, as though their journey into the next life has already begun. The hands, by contrast, are clumsily rendered, those of the anatomist excepted. It may be that they are the efforts of others, for Mier would not be alone among artists in allowing his students to complete his paintings. But then it could also be that it is Mier's intention to draw our gaze to the anatomist's hands. There is a grace, a subtlety to the scientist's calling, and Mier is perhaps suggesting that these are skilled fingers holding the blade.

To Mier, this is an artist at work.

III

I admit that I have never seen the painting in question. I have only a vision of it in my mind based upon my knowledge of such matters. But why should that concern us? Is not imagining the first step towards bringing something into being? One must envisage it, and then one can begin to make it a reality. All great art commences with a vision, and perhaps it may be that the vision is closer to God than that which is ultimately created by the artist's brush. There will always be human flaws in the execution. Only in the mind can the artist achieve true perfection.

IV

It is possible that the painting called *The Anatomisation of an Unknown Man* may not exist.

V

What is the identity of the woman? Why would someone force her to watch as a man is torn apart, compel her to listen to his screams as the blade takes him slowly, exquisitely apart? Surgeons and scientists do not torture in this way.

Thus, if we are not gazing upon a surgeon at work, then, for want of another word, we are looking at a murderer. He is older than the others in the picture, although not so old that his beard has turned grey. The woman, meanwhile, is beautiful; let there be no doubt of that. Mier was not a sentimental man, and would not have portrayed her as other than she was. The victim, too, is closer in age to the woman than the man. We can see it in his face, and in the once youthful perfection of his now ruined body.

Yes, perhaps he has the look of a Spaniard about him.

VI

I admit that Frans Mier may not exist.

VII

With this knowledge, gleaned from close examination of the work in question, let us now construct a narrative. The man with the knife is not a surgeon, although he might wish to be, but he has a curiosity about the nature of the human body that has led him to observe closely the attentions of the anatomists. The woman? Let us say: his wife, lovely yet unfaithful, fickle in her affections, weary of the aging body that shares her bed and hungry for firmer flesh.

And the man on the table, then, is, or was, her lover. What if we were to suppose that the husband has discovered his wife's infidelity. Perhaps the young man is his apprentice, one whom he has trusted and loved as a substitute for the child that has never graced his marriage. Realizing the nature of his betrayal, the master lures his apprentice to the cellar, where the table is waiting. No, wait: he drugs him with tainted wine, for the apprentice is younger and stronger than he is, and the master is unsure of his ability to overpower him.

When the apprentice regains consciousness, woken by the screams of the woman trapped with him, he is powerless to move. He adds his voice to hers, but the walls are thick, and the cellar deep. There is no one to hear.

A figure advances, and the lamp catches the sharp blade, and the grim work begins.

VIII

So: this is our version of the truth, our answer to the question of attribution. I, Nicolaes Deyman, did kill my apprentice Mantegna. I anatomised him in my cellar, slowly taking him apart as though, like the physicians of old, I might be able to find some as yet unsuspected fifth humour within him, some black and malignant thing responsible for his betrayal. I did force my wife, my beloved Judith, to watch as I removed skin from flesh, and flesh from bone. When her lover was dead, I strangled her with a rope, and I wept as I did so.

I accept the justice and wisdom of the court's verdict: that my name should be struck from all titles and records and never uttered again; that I should be taken from this place and hanged in secret and then, while still breathing, that I should be handed over to the anatomists and carried to their great temple of learning, there to be taken apart while my heart beats so that the slow manner of my dying might contribute to the greater sum of human knowledge, and thereby make some recompense for my crimes. I ask only this: that an artist, a man of some small talent, might be permitted to observe and record all that transpires so the painting called *The Anatomisation of an Unknown Man* might at last come into existence. After all, I have begun the work for him. I have imagined it. I have described it. I have given him his subject, and willed it into being.

For I, too, am an artist, in my way.

The Listening Room

by

ROBERT J. RANDISI

I

The best way for Truxton Lewis to warm up on a frigid January night in St. Louis was to experience some hot jazz at a new club called The Listening Room. Located on Del Mar, in the heart of University City, the club had been operating for only a month, and was owned by an old friend of his from his police department days.

The invitation had been extended to Tru Lewis from opening night on, but this was his first actual visit to the club. He was there because it was cold outside and hot inside, but also because the owner, Billy Danvers, had called him and asked him to come.

Tru had gotten the call that morning on his cell phone, while he was having breakfast in his new house in Bourbon, Missouri ...

"hey, tru?"

He recognized Billy's voice immediately, because it had a distinctive timbre to it. Billy Danvers had always had a great speaking voice. Rich in timbre, some women even called it beautiful. Because of that Billy had always wanted to be a singer—specifically, a jazz singer—but the problem was that when he opened his mouth to sing nothing beautiful ever came out.

"Billy?"

"Yep," Danvers said, "it's me."

"I've been meaning to come to your club, but—"

"That's why I'm callin', Tru," Billy said, cutting him off. "I know I invited you to come to the club and listen, but now I need you to come so I can talk to you. I'm havin' some problems, man."

"What kind of problems, Billy?"

"The kind you can help me with," Danvers said. "You were always the best cop I ever knew, Tru."

"So this is serious."

"Very serious. Can you come to the club tonight?"

"I'll be there, Billy. What time?"

"Come for the nine p.m. set and we'll talk after. I'm leavin' your name at the door and everything's comped."

"That's not necessary, Billy," Tru said, "but I'll be there."

"Thanks, Tru," Billy said. "It means a lot to me."

"I'll see you tonight," Truxton said.

FOR TRUXTON LEWIS the best thing about Bourbon, Missouri was that it only had about 1380 people, give or take ten. For a man who liked his privacy, this was a good size for a town to be. He'd house-sitted a four bedroom, two and a half bath with a finished basement and two car garage for about two weeks a few months back, and had fallen in love with the town. The people who had built this house had also liked Bourbon for its size. However, the home they had constructed seemed grossly out of place in a small city where the mean value of a home was $50,000. This house had to have cost a bundle to build, and when they decided to sell it they'd no doubt be asking close to $150,000.

But for Tru Lewis Bourbon was a haven, a place to hang his hat when he wasn't travelling around the country. Housesitting was a profession—no, more of a pastime—Truxton Lewis had taken on after the recent death of his wife of thirty years, and his retirement from the New York City Police Department after twenty-five. His daughter didn't like the new venture her father had taken up about a year ago, and she'd liked it even less when he announced he was moving to Missouri.

The bad thing about Bourbon was that it was seventy-five miles from St. Louis. That didn't sound like a lot, but while Truxton Lewis enjoyed travel he detested driving. His preferred mode of transportation was walking and, being from New York, he'd always made the best use of public transportation. He used to enjoy flying but that had ceased to be fun even before the 9/11 debacle in New York. Too many families with kids, or hockey teams or glee clubs or the idiots who went on spring break. Also bad meals—or meals of peanuts and pretzels—served by surly "flight attendants." He longed for the days of real meals served by pretty and attentive "stewardesses."

But those days were gone and if he was going to go into St. Louis to The Listening Room, he was going to have to drive. Upon his arrival in Missouri two months ago he'd purchased a used Toyota just to use locally. Any extensive travelling he would do would still be done by train or—when the need arose—by plane. Even more locally, in Bourbon, he'd walk.

He drove into St. Louis, taking I-44, and found his way to University City. He still didn't know St. Louis that well, and in fact had only been to the city a few times since moving to Bourbon. The small-town life had been what he'd been looking for when he left

New York. The big city held too many memories of his wife, and at sixty-three he was looking to start over again.

He had a computer in his small one-bedroom house which he'd gotten for a song—the house, not the computer—and had used Mapquest to get directions to the club. The Listening Room had a small parking lot and he claimed one of the remaining spots available and went inside.

The ambience was dark and warm as he stepped inside and gave his name to the man who was covering the door, clad in a tuxedo.

"Yes, sir, Mr. Lewis," he said, "we have your name right here. Will you be dining tonight?"

"No," Tru said, "I'm just here for the music." He'd had a fast-food dinner along the highway. Junk food was something else his daughter didn't approve of. Tru had eaten a lot of it as a street cop, but had gotten away from it as a detective. Now, later in life, he was starting to eat it again and was finding it much better than the first time around, cholesterol be damned.

The man turned and lifted his hand and a twentyish waitress appeared, very pretty in a crisp white shirt and black skirt.

"Amy will show you to your table," the man said. "Enjoy the show."

"Thank you."

He followed the waitress's saucy butt to his table, feeling his age as he did around girls her age.

"Would you like a drink?" she asked.

"Yes," he said, "beer. Whatever you have on tap that's local."

"That would be Schlafley's."

"Fine. What time does the show start?"

"Nine on the dot."

"And how long does it run?"

"Usually sixty to seventy minutes, depending on the performer."

"Okay, thank you."

"Mr. Danvers says you're comped, so if you want anything else just let me know."

"I will, Amy. Thanks."

She smiled and flounced away while Tru watched, feeling like a dirty old man.

II

Truxton took a moment to look the club over. It was a good-sized room with space between the tables. He knew some places would have pushed the tables closer together and sacrificed privacy for volume. He was glad his friend had chosen to go this way. The walls were dark wood and the tables were solid, with white cloths on them. When Amy came back with his beer it was in a traditional tapered glass, the way Tru liked it. So far he didn't see Billy Danvers skimping anywhere. Next time, he vowed, he'd sample the food. Tonight he was wondering what kind of problems Billy was having, and that would have interfered with his enjoyment of food.

As for the entertainment he had never before heard of the woman who was singing, but she was very good. He'd find out from Danvers if she was well known or not. As far as jazz was concerned he knew the historical names, Boots and Bird and Chet Baker. Of the new artists he only knew Harry Connick Jr. and Diana Krall. As for instrumentalists, his knowledge was limited to Kenny G and Candy Dulfer.

He was on his second drink by the time the lights went down and the woman came on stage. The stage was close, the room intimate. She had a piano player, a bass player and a drummer. At one point she even replaced the piano player for a couple of songs. She was good, entertaining, but nothing spectacular.

As she started a new song someone touched his shoulder from behind. He turned and looked into the face of his waitress.

"Mr. Danvers said I should send you back when she started her last song."

"Oh, okay."

"Follow me.'

He tried not to watch her tush while he followed her but then thought, "What the hell, I'm not dead."

"It's the door at the end of the hall."

He walked to the end of the hall, past several other doors, and knocked on the office door. When there was no answer he turned to look behind him, but Amy had moved on already. He knocked again, and when there was no answer tried the doorknob. It turned, so he opened the door and walked in.

"Billy—" he said, but that was as far as he got because the man seated at the desk in the leather chair had a silver letter opener sticking out of his chest. There was very little blood, but that didn't matter.

He was dead.

Truxton turned and hurried back down the hall. There was a good chance the murderer was still in the building and he knew that after the singer finished her last song people would start to leave.

He went to the front to the man who had let him in and grabbed his arm.

"Wha—"

"Your boss is dead," Tru said. "Somebody killed him. You can't let anybody leave, and you have to call nine-one-one."

"What the hell—who are you?"

Tru did something he didn't like to do. He took out his badge, which had the abbreviation "Ret." on it, but lots of people wouldn't notice that, and the doorman was one of them.

"Call nine-one-one, tell them a man's been murdered and give them the address."

"Jesus," the man said, "Mr. Danvers—"

"Yes," Tru said, "Billy Danvers, your boss, is dead. Now make the call—and remember, nobody leaves!"

"But how do I keep them all here?"

"You have bouncers, don't you?"

"Well … yeah, but—"

"Place them at the door," Tru said. "I don't care what it takes. Nobody leaves."

III

Tru went back to the office to wait, and that's where he was when the cops arrived. First he had to deal with the uniforms. He showed them his badge and they agreed to let him remain at the door of the room while one of them waited inside with the body and the other waited outside for the detectives.

"You might want to call for some backup. You'll need help keeping the crowd inside."

"Yes, sir," one of them said, "we intend to do that."

The detectives were next, a mismatched pair of men named Helmuth and Cloutier.

Helmuth, the youngest, had an attitude. Cloutier, in his fifties, with a head of steel-grey hair, looked at Truxton's badge closely.

"Retired?" he asked.

"Captain of Detective," Tru said.

Cloutier nodded and handed the badge back.

"Fill me in on the victim."

The body would not be moved until the M.E. arrived, so there was time.

"Billy Danvers. I knew him in New York. We were both cops together, came out of the academy together. He retired before I did, even though he's younger. He's always loved jazz and decided to become involved in that world. I don't know all that he's done in the past ten years, but it brought him here, to St. Louis, and to this club."

"And to this," Cloutier said, looking at the body behind the desk.

"That's a fairly heavy-duty letter opener," Tru said, "but it still must have taken a lot of strength to plunge it into his chest."

"You're thinking a man?"

"Or a hefty woman."

"Did you see any hefty women in the club tonight?" Cloutier asked.

"I'm afraid I was either looking at the woman on stage, or my waitress's butt."

"Can't blame you there," Helmuth said, with a smirk. "Probably all an old coot like you can do now is look, huh?"

Tru ignored the man, but the remark seemed to anger his partner.

"Go out front and wait for the M.E., Phil."

"Why do I have to—"

"Just go!"

Helmuth made an annoyed noise with his mouth and left the office.

"I'm sorry," Cloutier said, "he's young."

"I took that into account when he made the remark."

"You're more understanding than I am."

"I'm older."

"Not by much."

Cloutier turned back to the body. He and Tru were alone in the office. He started studying the photos on the walls.

"That's Bill Withers," he said, pointing, "and that's Lou Rawls. And Diana Krall! Are these photos genuine?"

They were framed and hanging on the wall, photos of Danvers with famous jazz artists. Cloutier examined the rest of the photos while Truxton looked around the room. He noticed the room smelled of something—freshener, or disinfectant. On the floor were two cigarettes, smoked halfway down and squashed flat.

"I can't say for sure," Tru said, "but knowing Billy I'd bet they were. It was his dream to meet those people, so I guess he did."

"Wouldn't mind meeting them myself," Cloutier said.

He turned around suddenly and looked at Tru.

"I'm sorry," he said. "You've lost a friend and I'm talking about jazz."

"I hadn't seen him in about five or six years, I think," Tru said. "I'm kind of … numb about the whole thing. We were friends in that we worked together for a while, but we certainly weren't close."

"You said he called and said he had a problem you could help him with?"

"That's right."

"He didn't say what it was?"

"Only that I could help because I was an ex-cop."

"He was an ex-cop," Cloutier said. "I wonder why he couldn't help himself?"

"I never got the chance to ask," Tru said. "I wish I'd insisted on seeing him as soon as I arrived. Maybe he'd still be alive."

"Can't berate yourself, Captain," Cloutier said. "How were you to know?"

"Not Captain," Truxton said. "You can call me Tru."

"Unusual name, Truxton."

"My parents were unusual people."

Helmuth stuck his head in the door and said with attitude, "M.E.'s here. Should I let him in?"

"We're waiting for him, aren't we, Phil?"

Helmuth withdrew without reply. Moments later an older man—older than Truxton—entered and raised bushy eyebrows at the body.

"Oh my," the M.E. said.

"Doctor Doyle, this is Captain Lewis, retired from the New York City Police Department. He's a friend of the deceased, found the body."

"Bad business," the doctor said. "I'm sorry for you."

"Thanks."

The doctor went to the desk and performed a brief examination of the body.

"Looks like the letter opener went right through the heart. He died instantly, not much blood." He turned and looked at Cloutier. "Can I have him?"

"If you're done with him here, so am I," Cloutier said.

"I'll have my boys come in and bag him."

"Let's get out of the way," Cloutier said to Truxton. "I've got to start questioning people. You want to sit in?"

"Why not?"

They started down the hall together. Tru noticed that two of the doors he'd passed earlier were rest rooms—men's and women's. Another door was unmarked.

"You mind if I open this?" he asked Cloutier.

"No, go ahead."

Tru opened the door and both men looked inside. It was a closet, with a broom, mop, bucket and room for a person or two.

"Think somebody waited in here for a chance at him?" Cloutier asked.

"No," Tru said, closing the door.

"Why not?"

"Because somebody waiting to kill him would have brought their own weapon," Tru said. "A letter opener, that's a weapon of opportunity."

"So you think this was ... unplanned?"

"Yes, I do," Tru said. "This looks like a spur of the moment killing. Maybe there was an argument, maybe the person felt threatened, grabbed the letter opener ..." Tru shrugged.

"Is there a back door, I wonder?"

"I don't know."

They continued back into the club, where people were sitting, and milling about, waiting impatiently to be allowed to go home. The singer and her group were seated on the stage, and she was smoking impatiently.

"We'll have to split them up, Phil," Cloutier said. "You question the staff, I'll start on the patrons. You can help me with them when you're done."

"What about the musicians?" Truxton asked.

"We'll treat them as staff, I guess."

"Why don't I pitch in and help?" Tru asked. "I'll question them."

"You don't have any authority here—" Helmuth started to say, but Cloutier cut him off.

"No, that's okay," he said. "We can use the help."

"You're in charge," Helmuth said.

"I'll take the heat, Phil," Cloutier said. "Why don't you get started."

"Fine," Helmuth said, and walked away.

"He might be right," Tru said. "Maybe I should just take a seat—"

"No, it's my call," Cloutier said, "and we're shorthanded. Go ahead, do it."

"Okay," Truxton said, "thanks."

Cloutier went off to do his part and start questioning patrons. He knew the detective would question them, then take their names and addresses and send them home. Once everybody was gone Billy Danvers' murder was going to be harder to solve.

He walked up to the stage where the singer was squashing a cigarette out in an ashtray. On the floor were two half-smoked cigarettes, squashed flat. Tru looked up at the four people on the stage—the singer, the pianist, the bass player, and the drummer. Sometimes, he thought, it's a matter of where you look. Cloutier had been looking at the pictures on the wall, not at the floor. Not at the scene.

"My name is Truxton Lewis," he said to the quartet. "I'm ... working with the police."

The singer looked at him. Up close he could see how heavy her makeup was. She also looked more fifty than forty this close up.

"You were in the audience," she said.

"Yes," he said. "I heard most of your set." For a moment he felt that he still couldn't recall her name.

"Carla Jenkins," she said, smiling. "You were trying to remember my name."

"I'm sorry."

"Don't be." She turned and pointed to the musicians. "Hal Joseph, Dave Malden and the bass player is Vic Cantone."

Truxton nodded to all three men. Hal, the drummer, was grey-haired, fiftyish, wearing a T-shirt and jeans. Vic was a young man, early thirties, wearing a suit and tie. Dave Malden looked forty, might have been fifty, was delicately built, probably didn't weigh one fifty. He had a sports jacket over a shirt buttoned to the neck. The other two men were over six feet.

"We heard the owner was murdered. Are we suspects?" she asked.

"At this point everyone is suspect."

"With him dead we may not get paid for this gig," she pointed out.

"That might not matter to the killer."

She laughed and said, "Matters to me."

"Who does the negotiating?" Tru asked.

"I do," Carla said. "I'm the headliner. The guys back me up."

"So you were in the office at some point?"

"Of course," she said. "That's where one does the negotiating."

"And none of you fellas have been in the office?"

"Nope."

"Never."

"Not me."

Truxton bent over and picked up the cigarettes from the floor of the small stage.

"Whose are these?" he asked.

"Not mine," she said, indicating the one she had just lit. "Mine are in the ashtray."

"They're mine," Hal, the drummer said. "What about it? It's not a non-smoking building, is it?"

"They're only smoked halfway down."

"I'm tryin' to quit," the man said.

"He smokes 'em exactly halfway," the woman said. "Doesn't want to miss a drag."

"Sit tight," Truxton said to them. "You might be able to go home, soon."

"What about getting paid?" Carla Jenkins asked.

"I can't help you with that."

He didn't bother pointing out that only three of them might be going home.

IV

There were four flattened cigarettes sitting on top of Billy Danvers' desk.

"These two," Truxton said to Detective Cloutier, "I took from the floor of the stage. These two, I took off of this floor."

"You brought us in here to show us cigarettes?" Helmuth asked.

"Very special cigarettes," Truxton said. He directed his comment to Cloutier, who was more receptive. Two things you've got to know about Billy Danvers. He was a clean freak. Can you smell it in here?"

Cloutier sniffed the air. "Cleaning solution of some kind."

"Right. I found two of these cigarettes right here on the floor in front of his desk. No way he'd leave those here."

"If he saw them," Cloutier said.

"Right."

"So chances are he was dead when whoever stomped out these cigarettes left the room."

"Chances are."

"But it's not certain," Helmuth said.

"Not at all," Truxton said, "but like I said, I found these other two cigarettes on the stage."

"Who smoked 'em?" Cloutier asked.

"The drummer."

"Don't mean he killed anybody," Helmuth said. "Just means he was in here."

"You're right," Tru said, "but all three of those men told me they weren't in here."

"So he lied," Cloutier said.

"He lied." Tru also told the detectives what he knew about the drummer—Hal Joseph—trying to quit smoking.

"So he smokes 'em all down to exactly the same place," Cloutier said.

"That's right."

The older detective turned to Helmuth.

"Bring the drummer in here," he said. "Let's see what he has to say for himself."

Helmuth, looking unhappy about it, said, "Yeah, okay."

After he left Cloutier passed a hand over his face and said, "I gotta retire. I missed those cigarettes."

"Could have happened to anyone."

"You got any idea why I agreed to let you help here?" the man asked.

"Crossed my mind."

"It's 'cause I'm losin' it, and I know it," Cloutier said. "Oh, I'm not sayin' I'm a bad detective. I've had my day, but I just don't have a taste for it anymore."

Truxton didn't know what to say, and was saved from saying something trite when Helmuth walked in with Hal Joseph.

"Have a seat, Mr. Joseph. My name is Detective Cloutier, this is my partner Detective Helmuth. I believe you've already met Mr. Lewis."

"What's this all about?"

Cloutier hesitated, then said, "I'll let Mr. Lewis answer that, since he's the one who spoke to you earlier."

"Is he a cop?" Joseph asked.

"He used to be."

"Then I don't have to talk to him, do I?" the drummer asked.

"Uh, yes, you do," Cloutier said. "Sit down. Phil, close that door."

Helmuth closed it and put his back to it.

"Truxton?" Cloutier said.

Tru, unprepared for Cloutier to hand the play over to him, stepped forward.

"Mr. Joseph, you told me you'd never been in this office."

"Did I say that?"

"Yes, you did," Tru said, "and yet I found these cigarettes on the floor tonight—smoked halfway down, and crushed underfoot."

"Lots of people crush cigarettes out under their feet," Joseph said. "Doesn't mean a thing."

"Are you still maintaining that you've never been in this office?"

The drummer hesitated, coughed into his hand, then said, "Okay, well, so, uh, maybe I've been in here before."

"Maybe you were in here tonight," Truxton said.

"Maybe," Cloutier said, stepping forward, "you stabbed Billy Danvers with this letter opener and killed him."

The detective held the letter opener in his hand, in a plastic bag. It was the first time Truxton had seen it out of Billy's chest. It had a heavy blade and a leather handle. A fancy instrument with which to open letters—and sturdy enough to kill.

Joseph stared at the letter opener in Cloutier's hand and said, "No."

"Then why don't you tell us what you were doing in here earlier tonight, Mr. Joseph," Truxton said.

"Look," Joseph said, "look … I didn't kill him. Okay, we had a little, uh, argument."

"About what?"

"Money."

"He owe you," Truxton asked, "or did you owe him?"

The man squirmed uncomfortably.

"Look," he said, "this goes back a ways. Billy used to be involved with a record label that I recorded on."

"How far back are we going?" Tru asked.

"Ten years, maybe more," Joseph said. "He ... lost the job because he got caught with his hand in the cookie jar."

"And some of the cookies were yours?" Cloutier asked.

"Huh? Oh, yeah, right. I was playing with a trio at the time and we felt he stole some money that belonged to us."

"So you thought you'd get it back from him tonight?" Truxton asked. "Is that why you took this job?"

"Yeah," he said. "When Carla called me and told me about this, she told me who the owner was. I figured I could get some of the money back from him. I—I'm not doin' as well as I once was."

"And how did you figure you'd get the money back?" Tru asked. "Just by asking nicely?"

"Well ... he owns his own club. I figured he had to have some money somewhere."

"So you asked him for it?"

"Sonofabitch said he didn't remember me," Joseph said. "But he did. He bitched about me smoking in his office, so I lit up two cigarettes just to piss him off."

"Not exactly the right way to go when you're asking for money, was it?" Cloutier asked.

"He'd already said no," Joseph said. "He told me he wasn't about to pay a debt he didn't remember."

"And then what?" Tru asked.

"And then I ... left his office."

"And he was alive?" Cloutier asked.

"Sittin' right there," Joseph said, indicating the chair the dead man had been in.

"Mr. Joseph," Truxton said, "I think there's something you're not telling us."

"Huh? Like what?"

"Where do you live?"

"Baltimore."

"You want us to believe you came all the way here from Baltimore to ask Billy Danvers for the money he stole from you, and when he refused to give it to you, you just walked out of his office?"

"That's what happened," Joseph said, "but I also came here for the gig. Carla calls me to play drums for her most of the time."

Cloutier looked at Truxton, obviously wondering what he had in mind. Helmuth, still leaning against the door with his arms folded, rolled his eyes.

"I think," Truxton said, "that since you feel certain Billy was skimming money from the record label you were signed with, that when he refused to give you any money you threatened him."

"Wha—no."

"I think you threatened to ruin his reputation here in St. Louis, which he couldn't afford since this club has only been open a month."

"Blackmail?" Cloutier said. Tru looked at him and nodded. "That makes sense," the detective said. He looked at Hal Joseph. "What about it? You want to cop to some attempted blackmail now so we don't find out about it later, when it'll really look like a motive?"

"Motive?" Joseph asked. "If I was tryin' to blackmail him, wouldn't that give him the motive to try and kill me?"

"And did he?" Truxton asked. "Did he grab the letter opener and try to use it on you, so that you had to defend yourself? Are you claiming self-defence, Mr. Joseph?"

"N-no, I'm not," the drummer said nervously. "Wait—"

"Wait for what, Mr. Joseph?" Cloutier asked. "Do you want a lawyer before you confess?"

"Confess? Wha—I'm not confessing."

"To what, Mr. Joseph?" Truxton asked. "Are you not confessing to murder, or to blackmail?"

"No, no, wait," the musician said, "you're confusing me. I am not confessing to murder."

"And what about blackmail?"

"Okay, okay," Joseph said, "I may have told him I was gonna spread it around town that he was a thief."

"If what?"

"If he didn't pay me."

"How much?"

"Ten thousand."

"Is that what you think he owed you?" Truxton asked.

"I—no, I figured ... you know ... with interest ..."

"If it's ten grand with interest, then it couldn't have really been much ten years ago, could it?" Truxton asked.

"It was the principle," Joseph said. "He shouldn't have stole anything!"

"So you made him pay the hard way, right?" Helmuth asked, springing away from the door. He grabbed the baggie containing the murder weapon from his partner's hand and waved it under Hal Joseph's nose. "You made him pay with his life!"

"No!"

"Come on, Joseph," Cloutier said. "Your cigarettes are on the floor, and I'll bet your fingerprints will be on the letter opener."

Suddenly, the man looked stricken. "Wait," he said, "wait ... when I first came in and sat he ... he asked me to hand him the letter opener."

"So you're saying your prints are on it," Truxton said.

"Well ... yeah, I guess ... b-but I never took it back from him. He held it the whole time."

"Did he ever threaten you with it?" Truxton asked.

"N-no—"

"Not even after you tried to blackmail him?"

"N-no, he never threatened me."

"You're full of shit, Joseph!" Helmuth said. He threw the plastic-encased letter opener onto the desk. "You're saying he never threatened you because that way you had no reason to defend yourself."

"Back off, Phil," Cloutier said.

"This asshole's lying," Helmuth said. "He did it."

"Maybe," Cloutier said, "but if the three of us keep yellin' at him he's not gonna be able to get a word in edgewise. Back off."

Reluctantly, Helmuth backed away.

"Why don't we three step outside and give the man time to think," Truxton suggested.

"Good idea," Cloutier said. "There's no other way out of here, anyway. Take five, Mr. Joseph. We'll be right back."

"Can I smoke?" the man asked.

"I think you've done enough damage to your credibility with your smoking, Mr. Joseph," Truxton said. "Try to hold off."

The three detectives left the room together after Truxton started to make a move for the desk but was waved off by Cloutier shaking his head.

Out in the hall Truxton said, "What did we get from the staff?"

"Not much," Cloutier said. "No one saw anybody go back to the office during the show."

"Billy must have been dead before the set started," Truxton said.

"The M.E.'s guess at time of death would support that."

"Hey," Helmuth said, "ain't we givin' him a chance to tamper with evidence, leavin' him in there alone?"

"What evidence, Phil?" Cloutier asked. "There was the body, which is gone, and the letter opener, which is—hey, where is it?"

"Don't worry, Phil," Cloutier said, "I've got—"

"Don't worry, hell!" Helmuth said. "He could be—" He cut himself off and charged into the room. Cloutier looked at Truxton, shrugged, and they went in after him.

"He wiped it clean!" Helmuth said, looking down at the letter opener in the bag. "See? It ain't sealed."

"Prove it!" Hal Joseph said. "I didn't touch it."

"Mr. Joseph," Cloutier said, "this is the letter opener you handed to Billy Danvers?"

"Yeah? So?"

"Well, if your prints are not on it now," Truxton said, "that would mean that you wiped it clean while we were in the hall. Why would you do that if you're not guilty?"

Hal Joseph looked trapped.

"I—I—oh, all right!" he said, finally. "I did it to protect Carla."

"Carla Jenkins?" Tru asked. "The singer?"

"That's right."

"You're sayin' the singer killed him with the letter opener?" Cloutier asked.

"That's what she told me," Joseph said. "She said they argued—Billy tried to put the moves on her, or something, I don't know—but they argued and she stabbed him."

"And he fell into the chair," Cloutier said.

"That's what she said," Joseph said. "I'm tellin' you. When you guys went outside I wiped off the letter opener to protect her."

"That's real noble of you Hal," Cloutier said, "except for one thing."

"What's that?"

Cloutier picked up the baggie with the letter opener and let the weapon drop out onto the desk.

"What're ya doin'—" Helmuth started.

"This isn't the murder weapon," Cloutier said. He took a baggie from his pocket with a silver letter opener in it—the one Truxton had seen sticking out of Billy Danvers' chest—and said, "This is."

"Wha—" Helmuth said.

"W-what? What?" Joseph stammered.

"I found that one in the desk drawer, and stuck it in a baggie," Cloutier said. "I wanted to see if you'd take the first opportunity to clean it off. See, now that you've told us that Carla Jenkins killed him, and all you did was touch the letter opener once to hand it to Billy Danvers, there should be three sets of prints on the murder weapon—the dead man's, yours and hers." Cloutier leaned over so his face was inches from Hal Joseph's. "If there's only two sets of prints—yours and his, and not hers—what do you think that means?"

"I—I—maybe she cleaned it—"

"You're the killer, Hal," Truxton said, "and you didn't have time to clean the murder weapon. Or maybe you couldn't bring yourself to do it while it was sticking out of Billy's chest. Either way, the fingerprints will tell the story—and so will Carla."

"She'll lie! She'll say she didn't do it—"

"You're the one who's lying, Hal," Cloutier said. He looked at Helmuth. "Cuff him and take him out."

Helmuth did as he was told, pouting the whole time that he hadn't been let in on the letter-opener switch.

"I thought you said you lost your taste for this," Truxton said. "That was a nice trick, switching the letter openers."

"You noticed right away, didn't you?"

"I knew the one sticking out of his chest had a silver handle. What if Joseph had remembered that, too?"

"I think we'll find out that the murder wasn't premeditated, and was probably a result of him trying to blackmail Danvers. They probably fought—whatever. I banked on him being flustered and not remembering the letter opener."

"Well, it was a good trick."

"You placed him in the room with those cigarettes," Cloutier said. "All I did was give him a chance to hang himself."

"When did you make a switch?"

"Right after the M.E. left and gave me the weapon. When I saw the second one I thought it might come in handy."

They left the room and walked down the hall together. Hal Joseph was already outside in a police car. Truxton looked at the stage and saw that Carla Jenkins was still smoking, and the other two men were staring off at the front of the club. They had to have seen Joseph being led out in cuffs.

"Should we tell them they'll need a new drummer?" Cloutier asked.

"I think they know."

"Do you think Danvers called you about the blackmail?"

"Couldn't have," Truxton said. "The call came yesterday, before Joseph tried it."

"What then?"

Truxton looked around The Listening Room, wondering what would happen to the place now. "I guess we'll never know."

Timber Town Justice

by

BARBARA FRADKIN

DR. DAVID BROWNE had scarcely been in town five minutes before he faced his first death. He had disembarked from the railway car and was standing on the platform in a daze, deafened by the rattle of carts on the planking and the hiss of venting steam. Sleet stung his eyes as he searched the harried throngs for a welcoming face.

Dr. Petley had assured him he'd be there with a carriage to transport him and his trunk to the boarding house. However, the train had been delayed so many times en route from Montreal that David had despaired of ever reaching civilization again. Even now, his first glimpse of Ottawa was hardly reassuring. A jumble of shabby huts, piles of lumber, and lanes of muddy slush.

All the horrors Liam had warned him of.

When he'd financed David's medical training, Liam had harboured lofty ambitions for his younger brother: a fashionable Sherbrooke Street practice, membership in the St. James Club, and a comely heiress on his arm at the latest charity ball. "Nation's Capital, nonsense!" Liam had fumed when David announced his decision to leave Montreal. "Nine years as the capital, and it's still nothing but a bawdy little timber town with an overblown Gothic chateau plopped in the middle."

Furthermore, at the moment even that wasn't visible through the sleet. David clutched his fur collar tighter and was turning in search of a porter when a commotion caught his eye. In front of him was Sussex Street cluttered with carts and carriages, beyond which the land dropped precipitously to the river below. He couldn't see over the bluff, but carriages had stopped and workmen were rushing toward the river.

"Some fool water carrier's fallen through the ice, no doubt," someone remarked.

"The river's not frozen yet," another countered. "No one's fool enough to go on it, especially near Rideau Falls!"

David snatched up his black bag, abandoned his trunk on the platform, and sprinted across the street. Down below he came upon a knot of labourers at the edge of the river. Two of the men had stripped off their coats to lay them on the ground and a crowd pressed around them, arguing in French.

David thrust forward. "Let me pass, I'm a doctor."

The crowd parted to reveal the bloodied body of a man spread out on the snow, his beard clotted with ice and his skull crushed above his left eye. A burly grey-bearded man was rubbing his frozen hands.

"I don't understand! He was just wit' us at the mill. Up at Chaudière."

David glanced anxiously up the river, but the legendary Chaudière Falls were out of sight. The man must have travelled in the freezing current quite a distance. He probed for a pulse. The man's skin felt icy but his heart was beating. Barely. David stripped off the wet clothing and wrapped his own fur coat around him tightly. "Where's the nearest warm building we can take him?"

"The Sisters' *hôpital* is not far," said the greybeard. "We bring him dere."

The two men carried the victim up to Sussex Street, where they intercepted a carter. After an animated exchange of French, they dumped their charge atop some sacks of potatoes. Directly David clambered up beside him, the carter snapped his reins, causing the horse to lunge forward. David cradled the injured man's head in his lap as they jolted over the icy ruts. With blood seeping slowly onto his waistcoat, he could almost hear Liam's bellows of protest ringing in his ears.

The man's eyes fluttered open and he gazed up at David through frosted lashes. *"Merci, monsieur."*

David permitted himself a faint hope. "What's your name? *Votre nom?*"

"Marc … Larivière." The man coughed up a pink foam that flecked his lips. David's faint hope faded.

"We're going to the hospital, Mr. Larivière. Just a little farther."

The man's eyes flickered. "No." He coughed again. "Please, home. *Je vous en prie.*"

His breath was growing laboured and his colour dusky. David, recognizing that he had probably passed beyond human help, acquiesced.

Larivière's destination was a two-room wood shack lit by a single candle and barely heated above freezing by a smoky, pot-bellied stove. Shooing her children out of the way, his wife pulled a straw mattress close to the stove so they could lay him down. Blood leaked out over the mat and David was appalled to discover angry welts all over his chest. How could rocks and ice have inflicted so much damage?

Although sensing the futility, he asked for hot water and more wood on the fire. Without hesitation the wife dispatched her oldest out the door with some coins from a jar.

"She cannot afford dat," the carter said to David.

"Wit'out him I afford not'ing," the wife retorted and turned to berate her husband in French.

Larivière tried to form words but no sound emerged, so he raised a feeble hand to summon her near. Still bristling, she put her ear close to his lips. His few tortured words caused her to stiffen in shock. The effort quite wore him out, for he collapsed in a paroxysm of coughing. Six pairs of solemn saucer eyes watched as he shifted his gaze from his wife to his children, took one last spasmodic breath, and expired.

Before David could react, a lanky young priest burst through the door. His glance travelled from the bed to the widow and thence to David, whereupon his eyes grew apprehensive.

"Am I too late? Is he dead?"

David deliberated. Like himself, the priest looked barely out of training, yet he was charged with the task of providing succour and healing far beyond his years. Although David was Anglo-Irish, he had grown up amid the wretched Irish-Catholic poverty of Griffintown and knew that faith had pulled many a spirit out of the mire. He stepped forward to feel the dead man's wrist before shaking his head. "He's failing, but still alive."

Gratitude shone in the young priest's eyes as he prepared for last rites. David suspected the priest recognized the deception, but they both understood the power of ritual. As he packed up his bag, the widow stopped him with a brusque hand. "*Combien, docteur?* How much?"

David contemplated the collection of straw mats by the wall and the single cast-iron cauldron on the stove, but before he could find an answer satisfactory to her pride, the priest spoke.

"Dr. St. Pierre charged five cents."

Five cents was so ludicrous that David feared if he had to follow St. Pierre's lead in all matters, he'd be in the poorhouse himself within a month. But the wife dug into the canning jar once again and handed over the coin with great dignity. Soon neighbours began to arrive, filling the house with the soft murmurs of condolence and the aromas of food. As David moved toward the door, the priest detached himself from the family and approached.

"May I accompany you to Sussex Street, doctor?"

Outside, David observed the streets for the first time. Most were crowded with modest wood houses, but in the distance could be seen the stone facades of more substantial buildings, dominated as in Montreal by the magnificent silver spires of a Roman Catholic church.

The priest picked his way up the street, his black robe sweeping the mud. "I'm Father Aubin," he began. "Thank you ... for that."

David hesitated, unsure how much to venture into a culture not his own. "That family ... Will there be help for them?"

A horse-drawn cart bearing a large wooden barrel drove by, splattering slush in its wake. The young priest leaped adroitly out of the way, a skill born of long practice, David concluded ruefully as he contemplated his own dirtied clothes.

"People will try," the priest replied in shy, accented English. "Marc Larivière was respected because he try to fight Jeremiah Wolfe for an acceptable wage. The sawmill owners reduce production when the markets are not favourable, but one must understand that for the people down here ..." He cast David a furtive look.

David completed the observation for him. "Five cents means they cannot heat their own homes."

Father Aubin blinked with relief. They had reached Sussex Street, which at this juncture was lined with brightly decorated shops, colourful wares, and elegant couples gliding arm and arm along the sidewalk. Balancing at the edge of the planking as if at the border of a foreign world, the priest extended his hand.

"I leave you here, Doctor. Perhaps we meet again?"

As David returned the handshake, he slipped the five-cent coin back into the other man's palm. "I think that house might need a little extra warmth tonight. A chill can bring on pneumonia when one's resistance is down."

THE WIDOW BARNABE's boarding house was situated on the south side of Sparks Street, affording an excellent view of the new Dominion's Parliament Hill. However, by the time David had supervised the unloading of his trunk, he was shivering so violently in his waistcoat that he scarcely paused to contemplate the splendour. Instead, he turned a grateful eye on the elegant Second Empire establishment that Dr. Petley had arranged for him.

His initial misgivings upon confronting the lumber piles of old Bytown gave way to relief. Even his brother would have no foundation for complaint, for the stately stone facades of Sparks Street rivalled the best of Sherbrooke Street. Widow Barnabe proved as lush and opulent as her domicile when she swept into the front hall in a trail of velvet and lace.

"We all feared you'd turned tail and fled! Dr. Petley has sent a boy over twice to inquire of your— Good heavens, what's happened!"

In the drama of the afternoon, David had quite forgotten his bloody clothing. When he explained, she clucked her tongue in dismay. "It's a devilish river that fools many a man. Raftsmen fall in, fishermen miscalculate the ice. And apart from that, the unsavoury elements are always throwing one another over the falls!"

She rang for the valet. "You must have a bath, and later I'll introduce you to the others. Drinks in the salon at seven, dinner at eight. Unless Dr. Petley spirits you away, of course. Poor fellow's been run off his feet since the city's expanded. What with the drains, the fires, the putrid water, and this eternal cold, it's a miracle any of us survive at all."

Fortunately, Dr. Petley did not spirit him away, but sent a message that he would call for David at ten o'clock the next morning. Unlike the dreary sleet of yesterday, the day dawned sunny and crisp, and when David gazed out his third-floor window he saw the copper spires of Parliament soaring over the rooftops. Eagerly he set out to enjoy a brisk morning stroll.

He had barely taken five steps when a black-robed figure detached from the shadows. "Dr. Browne? Can one talk?"

David started momentarily before recognizing the young priest from the previous day. Father Aubin's sparse beard quivered and his gaze flitted around the bustling street as he drew David into an alleyway. Garbage lined the walls and a suspicious brown slop oozed over David's boots, but such temporal concerns seemed to escape the priest entirely.

"Forgive me, Doctor," he began. "You seem a good man."

"Has something happened to the family?"

The father shook his head. "I do not know everything, you under-stand. But there must be a way to do something, to obtain justice for the family ..." He glanced out of the alley.

"What is it?"

"Marc Larivière was a raftsman before, and he knew the river. He was very careful. He wanted safety for the workers, not so long hours that they are always fatigued, not so small wage that they go to work hungry."

"I don't dispute that, Father. In Montreal I treated terrible accidents involving labourers. There have to be regulations."

Aubin nodded. "But the regulations, it is difficult to pass them. The workers do not have much votes."

David toyed with his walking stick restlessly. The stench and ooze were taking their toll on his patience, and the fresh breezes of Parliament Hill beckoned. "Shall we walk, Father? I'm anxious to make my acquaintance of this city."

Instead, the priest retreated still farther into the alley and lowered his voice to a whisper. "What happened was not an accident. Marc's wife tell me last night that before he died, he accused someone. She did not believe him, because Marc is fighting with this man and his friends since years. He blame them that wages go down. So she say to herself 'He just blame again. Many men lose their jobs. There is no wood to saw, nobody buy the wood they saw last year, and all Marc do is causing trouble.'"

David thought of the bruises on Larivière's body. "He accused someone of actually killing him? Another worker? One of the bosses?"

Father Aubin jerked his head back and forth, his beard quivering. "She could not be certain. She think he say Freddie O'Meara. He's a foreman at Chaudière."

"Why don't you tell the police?"

The priest looked appalled. "It's not easy. With no proof, only the word of a dying man. A poor man. A ..."

A Catholic and a Frenchman. Silently David furnished the thoughts the man did not dare voice aloud. In other words, a man considered little better than a savage, with no means to influence his lot. Although David was an Anglican and a member of the professional class, as a child growing up in Griffintown, he had known first-hand the humiliation of upper-class contempt.

At last David understood the reason for the priest's visit and the purpose he himself was to serve. By what unerring aim, he thought with despair, does trouble always find me so fast?

DAVID HAD NO SOONER RETURNED to the boarding house when a handsome brougham drew up to the door, bearing a large, florid man with a raccoon coat and a luxuriant red beard. Dr. Petley at last. The rest of the day was devoted to a tour of his surgery on fashionable Somerset Street, and of the new Protestant Hospital, where

David found the wards full of the labouring classes and the destitute. As in Montreal, families of means paid the physician to call at their house.

Dr. Petley strode through the hospital halls like a vice-regal, dispensing advice and good cheer in equal measure and being rewarded with smiles by even the most infirm. Despite the shiny glass cabinetry and fresh paint, many lay on straw mats on the floor.

"We're already overcrowded and most of these are non-paying," Dr. Petley said. "It's a challenge even in prosperous times to procure funds, but when economics are poor, the public institutions are the first to suffer."

After pausing to check a dressing on a young man's leg, he grunted with disgust. "We need properly trained nurses, not the illiterate chars we have at the moment. I've been thinking of opening a training school, but it's a devil of a time to get approval for anything in this city. If it's approved for the Protestants, the Catholics will protest, and if they get it, well, will it be Irish or French?"

He changed the dressing deftly before moving on. "Most of us devote a day a week here. Perhaps you can start with two days till your own practice is well established."

Up ahead, a straw mat blocked half the hall. On it a man was curled on his side with his arms hugging his abdomen. Dr. Petley bent to palpate the abdomen, then spoke sharply to the charwoman who was coming down the hall.

"Mrs. Watson! Where did this man come from?"

"That's Freddie O'Meara. Come in last night."

"Has anyone seen to him?"

"Dr. Graham, sir. When he were admitted. Broken jaw and rib, he said."

Dr. Petley's good cheer changed to pique in the blink of an eye. "Well, he's bleeding internally. He needs morphine. And find the poor fellow a quieter spot where everyone's not walking over him."

Thrusting her considerable bosom ahead like the prow of a ship, Mrs. Watson steamed off down the hall. Dr. Petley shook his head in exasperation. "She's of the view the unfortunate wretch is going to die anyway, so why trouble ourselves?"

"Die?" David looked at the patient with surprise. "But we could perform surgery. Perhaps repair the damage."

"Waste of time. Most of the patients die afterwards anyway."

"But with the new techniques ..." David perceived the complete bafflement on Dr. Petley's face and wisely chose a different course. "Have you any carbolic acid among the supplies?"

Grumbling about reckless extravagances, Dr. Petley reluctantly acceded to David's venture. The surgery theatre proved to be clean and well-equipped, and despite David's trepidation and Dr. Petley's ill-temper, the operation went smoothly. Afterwards, Freddie O'Meara was transferred to a clean bed in an empty isolation room, where David instructed the sullen Mrs. Watson on the changing of his dressing.

When David stopped in to check at the end of the day, he found Mrs. Watson engaging his groggy patient in banter.

"Well, Freddie my lad, you got yourself into a right altercation with your fists, you did."

O'Meara couldn't speak with his broken jaw, but she laughed as if his eyes held his answer.

"Sure you did. Someone wanted to finish you off proper this time. More's the pity he failed."

"Mrs. Watson!"

She started, but turned to give David a bold stare. "Evening, Doctor. You're new in town, so you won't know the O'Meara lads. Ruffians, the lot of them. Come down from Arnprior to work in the mills, and now when there's less jobs to go 'round, they got nothing better to do than the boss's dirty work."

Angrily David dispatched the woman to fetch a clean dressing and a bottle of carbolic. As a healer, neither the cause of his patients' injuries nor the comportment of their lives was of concern to him, yet according to the priest, Marc Larivière had implicated this young man in his violent and unjust demise. With Father Aubin's entreaty still fresh in his thoughts, David found his eyes drawn to O'Meara's hands. To his dismay, there was no mistaking the bruises and lacerations all across his knuckles.

WHEN DAVID ARRIVED back at the boarding house, he found Mrs. Barnabe supervising a crew of plasterers redoing the crown moulding in the salon. The small morning room was taken up with mountains of brocade and silk.

"The Governor General's fancy dress ball," came a lugubrious voice from behind a stack of chairs in the smoking room, where one of his fellow boarders was consoling himself with a generous measure of sherry. Rodney Sherwood was a young bachelor like David, and despite being the most junior addition to Giles and McIntosh Q.C.'s, was already possessed of a cynicism and girth to rival the senior partners'.

"The most excitement we've had since the Pacific scandal," he intoned with mournful glee. "Speculation has it that Lord Dufferin has invited fifteen hundred of *la crème de la crème,* and anybody who's anybody in this wretched country will be coming. Mrs. Barnabe expects to be cramming guests into the rafters."

"When is it?" David had visions of displaced furniture and plaster dust for months.

"Six weeks. The invitations have just arrived. Even the men are working themselves into a tizzy over what costume to wear. I encountered three Admiral Nelsons at court already today."

David poured himself a sherry, edged past a large bronze horse, and squeezed into a wing chair. "Does the Governor General have a ball every season?"

Sherwood waved the bottle his way. "His Excellency does love to bring on the trumpets and the jewels, but this will be his most ambitious affair by far. Designed to transform this erstwhile little timber town into London high society. The word is that half the lumber barons aren't even on the guest list. No spittoons at Rideau Hall."

The news surprised David, for the barons of industry were the backbone of Montreal society. "Are they not well regarded here?"

Sherwood shook his head with alacrity. "Too much dirt under their fingernails to suit the national image. Speaking of spittoons and dirty fingernails, Mrs. Barnabe told me you had quite an introduction to our fair city yesterday. You encountered one of Lower Town's famous river brawls."

Rodney Sherwood's obvious fondness for spirits and gossip gave David pause, but he needed someone with more knowledge of the city and the courts than he. "I'm concerned it may be something more sinister than a simple brawl. The poor man's head was crushed and it looks as if he may have been deliberately thrown over the falls. Have you ever heard of an Arnprior Irishman named Freddie O'Meara?"

"O'Meara?" the lawyer exclaimed. "If he's been tossed over the falls, the French will be lining up to claim the glory. He's been before the courts on half a dozen occasions for crushing heads, but witnesses were always in short supply."

In Montreal, David had treated dozens of factory workers beaten up or killed because they were trying to organize trade unions. In most cases, those responsible were in the employ of the factory owners. As he weighed Sherwood's words, his disquiet increased. Briefly he recounted Larivière's death and its possible connection to O'Meara. "Who does O'Meara work for?"

"He was just hired on by Jeremiah Wolfe, the biggest of the Chaudière barons." Sherwood swayed forward with sudden zeal. "Now *there's* a man who'd brook no opposition. Wolfe has ambitions far beyond a musty sawmill in a little backwater town, and woe betide any man who dares stand in his way."

"What ambitions?"

"He wants the new contract to build the Canadian Pacific Railway once this government finally decides to reinitiate it. Wolfe is convinced he can beat the St. Lawrence interests now that Sir Hugh Allan is disqualified."

"Then considering the taint left by that scandal, he must know his every action will be scrutinized. Surely he'd be a fool to engage the likes of Freddie O'Meara to kill someone for mere pennies in wages."

Sherwood wagged a wobbly finger. "Ah, but it's not simply wages, it's the rumour of labour upset. Won't do, with the railway already so far behind schedule. And Wolfe's a timber camp lumberjack, first and always, with a lumberjack's approach to settling accounts. He may be trying to insinuate his way into political and social favour, but the dirt under his fingernails is there to stay."

Drunken hyperbole aside, Sherwood's observation was unsettling enough that David sought to return the conversation to a lighter plane. "So no fancy dress ball for him, I wager."

"Certainly not if any collusion with O'Meara ever came to light. The doors at Rideau Hall would not only be slammed in his face, but locked and the key tossed into the drink. What's more, if Jeremiah Wolfe had a hand in this misadventure, I wouldn't give a York ha'penny for O'Meara's life right now."

DAVID DASHED DOWN the hospital corridor, clutching his black bag and jumping over patients asleep in the gaslit gloom. As he turned into Freddie O'Meara's room, he ran headlong into Dr. Petley, whose expression when he beheld David was considerably less amicable than it had been that afternoon. Behind him, Mrs. Watson was draping a sheet over the body on the bed.

"What happened?" David cried.

"Your patient died, Dr. Browne. I warned you it was a waste of your time. And mine, as it happened."

David turned to Mrs. Watson. "Were you watching him? Or did you simply leave him alone?"

The woman clamped her square jaw stubbornly, but Dr. Petley came to her defence. "Mrs. Watson has other duties to perform, Dr. Browne. I can assure you she sent for me the minute she found him. I've signed the death certificate, and now if you'll excuse me, I have a dinner engagement."

After his departure, David drew back the sheet to examine the body. The man was a desperate sight. His mouth gaped open and his skin was a cyanotic blue. David bent close to examine the eyes, then turned to Mrs. Watson aghast. "This man's been smothered!"

She backed away. "Don't look at me! I never touched him."

David gathered his composure with an effort, for he had seen the overcrowded conditions and the shortage of able-bodied assistants to attend the sick. "My reprimand was inappropriate, Mrs. Watson. I realize this is not your fault."

Her scowl eased. "Truth is, I'd check more often if I didn't have to be ten places at once. I had suppers to prepare and medicines to see to." She approached to stare at the body with a mixture of intrigue and distaste. "Smothered, eh? How can you tell?"

He pointed. "Do you see those little red spots all around the eyes? Those are tiny broken blood vessels. They occur in death due to asphyxia."

"I can't recollect …" She stopped, and David thought he detected a flicker of intelligence in her tiny, pig-like eyes. "You know, there were one man I seen going in this room. Just 'afore I went to dinner."

"What did he look like?"

"'Twere too dark in the hall. A workingman for sure. Dirty boots, grubby black beard."

"Would you recognize him again?"

"Oh, not in a month of Sundays. They all look alike, don't they, them mill workers. All covered in dirt and sawdust."

DAVID LAY AWAKE listening to the distant roar of the Chaudière Falls and the cacophony of snores through the thin walls. His thoughts whirled. Barely thirty-six hours had elapsed since he'd stepped off the train, yet what a quagmire he'd blundered into. Dr. Petley, who had been eagerly anticipating his arrival, now thought him a reckless incompetent. A young French priest had invested all his hopes in David's nonexistent influence with the city's elite. And now he was the sole possessor of knowledge of a double murder, with no hope of bringing to justice the man responsible. No witnesses, no evidence, and a death certificate from the senior doctor citing septic shock.

All night David despaired, but by dawn he had a plan.

At breakfast he penned a brief note and dispatched the stableboy to deliver it to the sawmill at Chaudière Falls. The boy came back by return tram with the answer. Mr. Jeremiah Wolfe would receive Dr. David Browne at two o'clock that afternoon.

Given his current meagre resources, David knew he ought to catch the city railway to Chaudière Island, but his mission demanded a dignity of bearing that a leap from the local horse car would not impart. Accordingly, at one-thirty he caught a cab along Sparks Street. The ride took him past luxurious mansions before descending a steep embankment and crossing a rickety wooden bridge into the shanty town of Lebreton Flats. Yellow sawdust blanketed the snow and the stench was appalling.

The cab headed across another bridge to the island, where limestone buildings, railway cars, and lumber piles occupied every inch of land. Halfway across, the cab halted in front of a building with a huge sign over its transom: WOLFE'S LUMBER AND RAIL COMPANY. David paid the cab and disembarked, more than fifteen minutes early.

The roar and the foaming fury of Chaudière Falls caught his attention instantly. Curious, he walked along the edge of the river to the falls. The water plunged off a semi-circular shelf and roiled in the pit below, tossing angrily to and fro before finding its escape downstream.

David studied the area carefully. Because of the season, there was no logging on the river itself, but narrow plankways crisscrossed the water above the falls. The area was screened by the sawmill's massive stone walls, permitting many a dispute to be settled here with a quick push, beyond sight or hearing of the workers nearby.

"Can I be of assistance?" a voice thundered.

David spun around to see a black-bearded titan bearing down on him, resplendent in bearskin coat and top hat. Instinctively David knew this was Jeremiah Wolfe. He straightened his spare frame, smoothed his own lamentably sparse beard, and introduced himself.

"I was early for our appointment and being new in town, decided to see for myself the legendary Big Kettle."

Wolfe said nothing, a man clearly not interested in the exchange of petty civilities, but merely fixed David with a bald stare. A jagged white scar ran the length of his cheek, testament to his brutal past. Flustered, David took the next step of his carefully rehearsed plan.

"And in truth," he added, "I'd been in town less than five minutes when I had to tend to an unfortunate fellow who was presumed to have fallen in here. Given the grievous nature of his injuries, I was anxious to view the surroundings for myself, to determine if there were hazards which perhaps I could undertake to address in the future. In the interests of public safety."

Wolfe's eyes narrowed beneath bushy brows. He cast his gaze out over the walkways and up the river. "It's dangerous work. The men who work here take pride in the battle they wage with the river."

"Without doubt." David nodded toward the main door. "I appreciate your granting me an audience so promptly, Mr. Wolfe, and I promise not to take much of your time."

If Wolfe harboured any private curiosity as to the reason for David's sudden overture, he betrayed none. Clasping his hands behind his back, he strode up the path at a pace that left David scrambling. "You're from Montreal, Dr. Browne?" he began and before David could fully register that he must have made inquiries, he went further. "Brother of Liam Browne, the woollen merchant, and son of Joseph Browne, the drunken shanty Irishman."

David tripped on the uneven stones, his cheeks flushing hot, but when he glanced at Wolfe, he saw a faint twinkle in the man's sharp eyes. "Just so we recognize each other."

David was grateful for the few moments to collect himself while Wolfe led the way to his rugged oak-panelled office and poured them both a strong shot of Scotch whisky. Your plan is not ruined, David reassured himself. Act in command, and you will be.

"You're right," he said once they had toasted the Queen's health. "I do have humble beginnings. I grew up in circumstances not far removed from those workers in Lower Town. As a physician, I consider that a blessing, and to be candid, the matter I wish to discuss with you concerns the wretched circumstances of one of those families. That unfortunate fellow I tended died from his wounds. He was one of your workers and I presume he died trying to fulfill his duties in your employ."

"Most regrettable, doctor," Wolfe observed. "I take every precaution with my men, but as I mentioned, the river can be a savage foe. I cannot be held responsible every time she wins."

"I concur. Unfortunately some foes are unforeseen, and it is his family who are paying the cost. He left a widow and six young children destitute in an unheated wood hovel in Lower Town."

"Rest assured, Dr. Browne, those people have their charitable organizations for the needy: the Church, the Sisters of Charity, and the St. Vincent de Paul Society, to which I contribute handsomely, I might add."

"Subsistence and hand-outs can't make up for the warmth, security, and support of a gainfully employed father, Mr. Wolfe. I know."

Wolfe's tone acquired a distinct chill. "What are you proposing, doctor?"

"A widow's allowance, enough to guarantee the family a comfortable home and provision for their future. It would mean mere pennies to you, but a lifeline to them."

Wolfe eyed him as if he'd taken leave of his senses. "If I paid a widow's allowance for every man lost on the job, I'd be bankrupt in a year."

"Not every man," David replied carefully. "Just this man. Because he fell to his death at your mill."

As the silence lengthened, David could almost see Wolfe working to maintain a civil tongue. "I wish I could help this family and all the other innocent children I see in the streets. But my role in the economic scheme is to build a great city. It is to foster growth, prosperity, and jobs so that all men of honour can support their families with pride. Charity would be perceived as weakness on my part, and the lazy and indigent would be lined up at my door."

David breathed deeply, uttering a silent prayer. "I have a way."

Wolfe's benevolence slipped briefly, but he smiled. More a baring of teeth than a smile, but an attempt nonetheless. "Do you?"

"Yesterday I made my first rounds at the new Protestant Hospital on Rideau Street. I found the conditions lamentable. The rooms are overcrowded, the staff inadequately trained, and the medical practices out of date. I encountered a patient who had been beaten almost to death—also a man in your employ, as it happens. I performed an operation using the new principles of antisepsis, and despite the alarming ignorance and overwork of the staff, the man should have recovered. Curiously, he did not."

Wolfe's smile vanished and his eyes grew shrewd. "And you propose …?"

"If you were to make a generous financial commitment to the Protestant Hospital, I would arrange to have a modest monthly sum set aside quietly for the widow Larivière. With the remainder, perhaps the hospital board might be persuaded to institute a school of nursing like the one being proposed at the Montreal General."

Wolfe sipped his Scotch. Stroked his beard. "And for my generosity, I would receive what?"

"The respect and gratitude of the entire community, sir. No small reward in a town where the recipients of your largesse might be parliamentarians and ministerial aides in sudden dire need of the latest medical help."

Slowly but surely Wolfe's smile returned, encouraging David sufficiently to venture his final flourish. "It might even be worth an invitation to the Governor General's fancy dress ball."

Wolfe threw his massive head back in a laugh. "And how much is this invitation going to cost me?"

"That, sir, is entirely up to your own generosity." David hesitated fractionally. "And your conscience."

Wolfe froze and David held his breath. He offered no explanation, no mitigation, merely left his words to linger in the air. After an apparent eternity, Wolfe reached for his cheque book.

Ten minutes later David stepped out the front door and into the brougham waiting at the curb. He paused for one final look, first at the wrath of the Big Kettle and then at the lacy silhouette of Parliament high on the bluff above. He felt equal measures of fear, horror, and exhilaration at his audacity. It might take awhile, but he was beginning to get the notion of how things operated in this timber town.

Triangle

by

JEFFERY DEAVER

"MAYBE I'LL GO to Baltimore."

"You mean …" She looked at him. "To see …"

"Doug," he answered.

"Really?" Mo Anderson asked and looked carefully at her fingernails, which she was painting bright red. He didn't like the colour but he didn't say anything about it. She wouldn't listen to him anyway.

"I think it'd be fun," he continued.

"Oh, it would be," she said quickly. "Doug's a fun guy."

"Sure is," Pete Anderson said. He sat across from Mo on the front porch of their split-level house in suburban Westchester County. The month was June and the air was thick with the smell of the jasmine that Mo had planted earlier in the spring. Pete used to like that smell. Now though it made him sick to his stomach.

Mo inspected her nails for streaks and pretended to be sort of bored with the idea of him going to see her friend Doug. But she was a lousy actor; Pete could tell she was really excited by the idea, and he knew why. But he just watched the lightning bugs and kept quiet. Unlike Mo, he *could* act.

"When would you go?" she asked.

"This weekend, I guess. Saturday."

They were silent and sipped their drinks, the ice clunking dully on the plastic glasses. It was the first day of summer and the sky wasn't completely dark yet even though it was nearly nine o'clock in the evening. There must've been a thousand lightning bugs in their front yard.

"I know I kinda said I'd help you clean up the garage," he said, wincing a little, looking guilty.

"No, I think you should go. I think it'd be a good idea," she said.

I *know* you think it'd be a good idea, Pete thought. But he didn't say this to her. Lately he'd been thinking a lot of things and not saying them.

Pete was sweating—more from excitement than from the heat— and he wiped the sweat off his face and around his buzz-cut blond hair with his napkin.

The phone rang and Mo went to answer it.

She came back and said, "It's your *father*," in that sour voice of hers that Pete hated. She sat down and didn't say anything else, just picked up her drink and examined her nails again.

Pete got up and went into the kitchen. His father lived in Wisconsin, not far from Lake Michigan. He loved the man and wished they lived closer together. Mo, though, didn't like him one bit and always raised a stink when Pete wanted to go visit. She never went with him. Pete was never exactly sure what the problem was between Mo and his dad. But it made him mad that she treated the man so badly and would never talk to Pete about it.

And he was mad too that Mo seemed to put Pete in the middle of things. Sometimes Pete even felt guilty he *had* a father.

He had a nice talk but hung up after only ten minutes because he felt Mo didn't want him to be on the phone.

Pete walked out onto the porch.

"Saturday," Mo said. "I think Saturday'd be fine."

Fine …

Then she looked at her watch and said, "It's getting late. Time for bed."

And when Mo said it was time for bed, it was definitely time for bed.

LATER THAT NIGHT, when Mo was asleep, Pete walked downstairs into the office. He reached behind a row of books resting on the built-in bookshelves and pulled out a large, sealed envelope.

He carried it down to his workshop in the basement. He opened the envelope and took out a book. It was called *Triangle* and Pete had found it in the True Crime section of a local used book shop after flipping through nearly twenty books about real-life murders. Pete had never ripped off anything, but that day he'd looked around the store and slipped the book inside his windbreaker then strolled casually out of the store. He'd *had* to steal it; he was afraid that—if everything went as he'd planned—the clerk might remember him buying the book and the police would use it as evidence.

Triangle was the story of a couple in Colorado Springs. The wife was married to a man named Roy. But she was also seeing another man—Hank—a local carpenter. Roy found out and waited until Hank was out hiking on a mountain path, then he snuck up beside him and pushed him over the cliff. Hank grabbed onto a tree root but he lost his grip—or Roy smashed his hands; it wasn't clear—and Hank fell a hundred feet to his death on the rocks in the valley. Roy went back home and had a drink with his wife just to watch her reaction when the call came that Hank was dead.

Pete didn't know squat about crimes. All he knew was what he'd seen on TV and in the movies. None of the criminals in those shows seemed very smart and were always getting caught by the good guys, even though *they* didn't really seem much smarter than the bad guys. But that crime in Colorado was a smart crime. Because there were no murder weapons and very few clues. The only reason Roy got caught was that he'd forgotten to look for witnesses.

If the killer had only taken the time to look around him, he would have seen the witnesses: A couple of campers had a perfect view of Hank Gibson plummeting to his bloody death, screaming as he fell, and of Roy standing on the cliff, watching him ...

Triangle became Pete's bible. He read it cover to cover—to see how Roy had planned the crime and to find out how the police had investigated it.

Tonight, with Mo asleep and his electronic airline ticket to Baltimore bought and paid for, Pete read *Triangle* once again, paying particular attention to the parts he'd underlined. Then he walked back upstairs, packed the book in the bottom of his suitcase and lay on the couch in the office, looking out the window at the hazy summer stars and thinking about his trip from every angle.

Because he wanted to make sure he got away with the crime. He didn't want to go to jail for life—like Roy.

Oh, sure there were risks. Pete knew that. But nothing was going to stop him.

Doug had to die.

Pete realized he'd been thinking about the idea, in the back of his mind, for months, since not long after Mo met Doug.

She worked part time for a drug company in Westchester—the same company Doug was a salesman for, assigned to the Baltimore office. They met when he came to the headquarters for a sales conference. Mo had told Pete that she was having dinner with "somebody" from the company but she didn't say who. Pete didn't think anything of it until he overheard her tell one of her girlfriends on the phone about this interesting guy she'd met. But then she realized Pete was standing near enough to hear and she changed the subject.

Over the next few months Pete realized that Mo was getting more and more distracted, paying less and less attention to him. And he heard her mention Doug more and more.

One night Pete asked her about him.

"Oh, Doug?" she said, sounding irritated. "Why, he's just a friend, that's all. Can't I have friends? Aren't I allowed?"

Pete noticed that Mo was starting to spend a lot of time on the phone and online. He tried to check the phone bills to see if she was calling Baltimore but she hid them or threw them out. He also tried to read her emails but found she'd changed her passcode. Pete was an expert with computers and easily broke into her account. But when he went to read her emails he found she'd deleted them all.

He was so furious he nearly smashed the computer.

Then, to Pete's dismay, Mo started inviting Doug to dinner at their house when he was in Westchester on company business. He was older than Mo and sort of heavy. But Pete admitted he was handsome and real slick. Those dinners were the worst ... They'd all three sit at the dinner table and Doug would try to charm Pete and ask him about computers and sports and the things that Mo obviously had told Doug that Pete liked. But it was real awkward and you could tell he didn't give a damn about Pete. He just wanted to be there with Mo, alone.

By then Pete was checking up on Mo all the time. Sometimes he'd pretend to go to a game with Sammy Biltmore or Tony Hale but he'd come home early and find that she was gone too. Then she'd come home at eight or nine and look all flustered, not expecting to find him, and she'd say she'd been working late even though she was just an office manager and hardly ever worked later than five before she met Doug. Once, when she claimed she was at the office, Pete found

Doug's number in Baltimore, and the message said he'd be out of town for a couple of days.

Everything was changing. Mo and Pete would have dinner together but it wasn't the same. They didn't have picnics and they didn't take walks in the evenings. And they hardly ever sat together on the porch anymore and look out at the fireflies and make plans for trips they wanted to take.

"I don't like him," Pete said. "Doug, I mean."

"Oh, quit being so jealous. He's a good friend, that's all. He likes both of us."

"No, he doesn't like me."

"Of course he does. You don't have to worry."

But Pete did worry, and he worried even more when he found a piece of paper in her purse last month. It said, *D. G.—Sunday, motel 2 p.m.*

Doug's last name was Grant.

That Sunday morning Pete tried not to react when Mo said, "I'm going out for a while, honey."

"Where you going?"

"Shopping. I'll be back by five."

He thought about asking her exactly where she was going, but he didn't think that was a good idea. It might make her suspicious. So he said cheerfully, "Okay, see you later."

As soon as her car had pulled out of the driveway he'd started calling motels in the area and asking for Douglas Grant.

The clerk at the Westchester Motor Inn said, "One minute, please. I'll connect you."

Pete hung up fast.

He was at the motel in fifteen minutes and, yep, there was Mo's car parked in front of one of the doors. Pete snuck up close to the room. The shade was drawn and the lights were out but the window was partly open. Pete could hear bits of the conversation.

"I don't like that."

"That ...?" she asked.

"That colour. I want you to paint your nails red. It's sexy. I don't like that colour you're wearing. What is it?"

"Peach."

"I like bright red," Doug said.

"Well, okay."

There was some laughing. Then a long silence. Pete tried to look inside but he couldn't see anything. Finally, Mo said, "We have to talk. About Pete."

"He knows something," Doug was saying. "I know he does."

"He's been like a damn spy lately," she said, with that edge to her voice that Pete hated. "Sometimes I'd like to strangle him."

Pete closed his eyes when he heard Mo say this. Pressed the lids closed so hard he thought he might never open them again.

He heard the sound of a beer can opening.

Doug said, "So what if he finds out?"

"So *what*? I told you what having an affair does to alimony in this state. It *eliminates* it. We have to be careful. I've got a lifestyle I'm accustomed to."

"Then what should we do?" Doug asked.

"I've been thinking about it. I think you should do something with him."

"Do something with him?" Doug had an edge to his voice too. "Get him a one-way ticket ..."

"Come on."

"Okay, sorry. But what do mean by do something?"

"Get to know him."

"You're kidding."

"Prove to him you're just a friend."

Doug laughed and said in a soft, low voice, "Does *that* feel like I'm just a friend?"

She laughed too. "Stop it. I'm trying to have a serious talk here."

"So, what? We go to a ball game together?"

"No, it's got to be more than that. Ask him to come visit you."

"Oh, that'd be fun." With that same snotty tone that Mo sometimes used.

She continued, "No, I like it. Ask him to come down. Pretend you've got a girlfriend or something."

"He won't believe that."

"Pete's only smart when it comes to computers and baseball. He's stupid about everything else."

Peter wrung his hands together. Nearly sprained a thumb—like the time he jammed his finger on the basketball court.

"That means I have to pretend I like him."

"Yeah, that's *exactly* what it means. It's not going to kill you."

"You come with him."

"No," she said. "I couldn't keep my hands off you."

A pause. Then Doug said, "Oh, hell, all right. I'll do it."

Pete, crouching on a strip of yellow grass beside three discarded soda cans, curled into a ball and shook with fury. It took all his willpower not to scream.

He hurried home, threw himself down on the couch in the office and turned on the game.

When Mo came home—which wasn't at five at all, like she promised, but at six-thirty—he pretended he'd fallen asleep.

That night he decided what he had to do, and the next day he went to the used book store and stole the copy of *Triangle*.

ON SATURDAY Mo drove him to the airport.

"You two gonna have fun together?" In the car she lit a cigarette. She'd never smoked before she met Doug.

"You bet," Pete said. He sounded cheerful because he *was* cheerful. "We're gonna have a fine time."

On the day of the murder, while his wife and her lover were sipping wine in a room at the Mountain View Lodge, Roy had lunch with a business associate. The man, who wished to remain anonymous, reported that Roy was in unusually good spirits. It seemed his depression had lifted and he was happy once more.

Fine, fine, fine ...

At the gate Mo kissed him and then hugged him hard. He didn't kiss her but he hugged her back. But not hard. He didn't want to touch her. Didn't want to be touched by her.

"You're looking forward to going, aren't you?" she asked.

"I sure am," he answered. This was true.

"I love you," she said.

"I love you too," he responded. This was not true. He hated her. He hoped the plane left on time. He didn't want to wait here with her any longer than he had to.

But the flight left as scheduled.

The flight attendant, a pretty blond woman, kept stopping at his seat. This wasn't unusual for Pete. Women liked him. He'd heard a million times that he was cute. Women were always leaning close and telling him that. Touching his arm, squeezing his shoulder. But today he answered her questions with a simple "yes" or "no." And kept reading *Triangle*. Reading the passages he'd underlined. Memorizing them.

Learning about fingerprints, about interviewing witnesses, about footprints and trace evidence. There was a lot he didn't understand, but he did figure out how smart the cops were and that he'd have to be very careful if he was going to kill Doug.

"We're about to land," the flight attendant said, "could you put your seatbelt on, please?"

She squeezed his shoulder and smiled at him.

He put the seatbelt on and went back to his book.

Hank Gibson's body had fallen one hundred and twelve feet. He'd landed on his right side, and of the more than two hundred bones in the human body, he'd broken seventy-seven. His ribs had pierced all his major internal organs and his skull was flattened on one side.

"Welcome to Baltimore, where the local time is twelve twenty-five," the flight attendant said. "Please remain in your seat with the seat belt fastened until the plane has come to a complete stop and the pilot has turned off the fasten seat belt sign. Thank you."

The medical examiner estimated that Hank was travelling eighty miles an hour when he struck the ground and that death was virtually instantaneous.

Welcome to Baltimore …

DOUG MET HIM at the airport. Shook his hand.

"How you doing, buddy?" Doug asked.

"Okay."

This was so weird. Spending the weekend with a man that Mo knew so well and that Pete hardly knew at all.

Going hiking with somebody he hardly knew at all.

Going to kill somebody he hardly knew at all …

He walked along beside Doug.

"I need a beer and some crabs," Doug said as they got into his car. "You hungry?"

"Sure am."

They stopped at the waterfront and went into an old dive. The place stunk. It smelled like the cleanser Mo used on the floor when Randolf, their Labrador retriever puppy, made a mess on the carpet.

Doug whistled at the waitress before they'd even sat down. "Hey, honey, think you can handle two real men?" He gave her the sort of grin he'd seen Doug give Mo a couple times. Pete looked away, somewhat embarrassed but plenty disgusted.

When they started to eat he calmed down, though that was more likely the beers. Like Mo got after her third glass of Gallo in the evenings. Doug had at least three that Pete counted and maybe a couple more after them.

Pete wasn't saying much. Doug tried to be cheerful. He talked and talked but it was just garbage. Pete didn't pay any attention.

"Maybe I'll give my girlfriend a call," Doug said suddenly. "See if she wants to join us."

"You have a girlfriend? What's her name?"

"Uhm, Cathy," he said.

The waitress's name tag said, *Hi, I'm Cathleen.*

"That'd be fun," Pete said.

"She might be going out of town this weekend." He avoided Pete's eyes. "But I'll call her later."

Pete's only smart when it comes to computers and baseball. He's stupid about everything else.

Finally Doug looked at his watch and said, "So what do you feel like doing now?"

Pete pretended to think for a minute and asked, "Anyplace we can go hiking around here?"

"Hiking?"

"Like any mountain trails?"

Doug finished his beer, shook his head. "Naw, nothing like that I know of."

Pete felt rage again—his hands were shaking, the blood roaring in his ears—but he covered it up pretty well and tried to think. Now, what was he going to do? He'd counted on Doug agreeing to whatever he wanted. He'd counted on a nice high cliff.

But then Doug continued. "But if you want to be outside, one thing we could do maybe is go hunting."

"Hunting?"

"Nothing good's in season now," Doug said. "But there's always rabbits and squirrels."

"Well—"

"I've got a couple guns we can use."

Guns?

Pete said, "Okay. Let's go hunting."

"YOU SHOOT MUCH?" Doug asked him.

"Some."

In fact, Pete was a good shot. His father had taught him how to load and clean guns and how to handle them. ("Never point it at anything unless you're prepared to shoot it.")

But Pete didn't want Doug to know he knew anything about guns, so he let the man show him how to load the little .22 and how to pull the slide to cock it and where the safety was.

I'm a *much* better actor than Mo.

They were in Doug's house, which was pretty nice. It was in the woods and it was a big house, all full of stone walls and glass. The furniture wasn't like the cheap things Mo and Pete had. It was mostly antiques.

Which depressed Pete even more, made him angrier, because he knew that Mo liked money and she liked *people* who had money even if they were idiots, like Doug. When Pete looked at Doug's beautiful house he knew that if Mo ever saw it she'd want Doug even more. Then he wondered if she *had* seen it. Pete had gone to Wisconsin a few months ago. Maybe Mo had come down here to spend the night with Doug.

"So," Doug said. "Ready?"

"Where're we going?" Pete asked.

"There's a good field about a mile from here. It's not posted. Anything we can hit we can take."

"Sounds good to me," Pete said.

They got into the car and Doug pulled onto the road.

"Better put that seatbelt on," Doug warned. "I drive like a crazy man."

THE FIELD LOOKED familiar to Pete.

As Doug laced up his boots, Pete realized why it was familiar. It was almost identical to a field in White Plains—the one across the highway from the elementary school. The only difference was that this one was completely quiet; the New York field was noisy. You heard a continual stream of traffic.

Pete was looking around.

Not a soul.

"What?" Doug asked, and Pete realized that the man was staring at him.

"Pretty quiet."

And deserted. No witnesses.

"Nobody knows about this place. I found it by my little old lonesome." Doug said this real proud, as if he'd discovered a cure for cancer. "Lessee." He lifted his rifle and squeezed off a round.

Crack …

He missed a can sitting about thirty feet away.

"Little rusty," he said. "But, hey, aren't we having fun?"

"Sure are," Pete answered.

Doug fired again, three times, and hit the can on the last shot. It leapt into the air. "There we go!"

Doug reloaded and they started through the tall grass and brush. They walked for five minutes.

"There," Doug said. "Can you hit that rock over there?"

He was pointing at a white rock about twenty feet from them. Pete thought he could have hit it, but he missed on purpose. He emptied the clip.

"Not bad," Doug said. "Came close the last few shots." Pete knew he was being sarcastic.

"So, what? We go to a ball game together?"

"No, it's got to be more than that. Ask him to come visit you."

"Oh, that'd be fun."

Pete reloaded and they continued through the grass.

"So," Doug said. "How's she doing?"

"Fine. She's fine."

Whenever Mo was upset and Pete'd ask her how she was she'd say, "Fine. I'm fine."

Which didn't mean fine at all. It meant, I don't feel like telling you anything. I'm keeping secrets from you.

They stepped over a few fallen logs and started down a hill. The grass was mixed with blue flowers and daisies. Mo liked to garden and was always driving up to the nursery to buy plants. Sometimes she'd come back without any and Pete began to wonder if, on those trips, she was really seeing Doug instead. He got angry again. Hands sweaty, teeth grinding together.

"She get her car fixed?" Doug asked. "She was saying that there was something wrong with the transmission."

How'd he know that? The car broke down only four days ago. Had Doug been there and Pete didn't know it?

Doug glanced at Pete and repeated the question.

Pete blinked. "Oh, her car? Yeah, it's okay. She took it in and they fixed it."

But then he felt better because that meant they *hadn't* talked yesterday or otherwise she would have told him about getting the car fixed.

On the other hand, maybe Doug was lying to him now. Making it *look* as if she hadn't told him about the car when they really had talked.

Pete looked at Doug's pudgy face and couldn't decide whether to believe him or not. He looked sort of innocent, but Pete had learned that people who seemed innocent were sometimes the most guilty. Roy, the husband in the *Triangle* book, had been a church choir director. From the smiling picture in the book, you'd never guess he'd kill a soul.

Thinking about the book, thinking about murder.

Pete was scanning the field. Yes, there ... about fifty feet away. A fence. Five feet high. It would work just fine.

Fine ...

As fine as Mo.

Who wanted Doug more than she wanted Pete.

"What're you looking for?" Doug asked.

"Something to shoot."

And thought: Just witnesses. That's all I'm looking for.

"Let's go that way," Pete said and walked toward the fence.

Doug shrugged. "Sure. Why not?"

Pete studied it as they approached. Wood posts about eight feet apart, five strands of rusting wire.

Not too easy to climb over, but it wasn't barbed wire like some of the fences they'd passed. Besides, Pete didn't want it *too* easy to climb. He'd been thinking. He had a plan.

Roy had thought about the murder for weeks. It had obsessed his every waking moment. He'd drawn charts and diagrams and planned every detail down to the nth degree. In his mind, at least, it was the perfect crime.

Pete now asked, "So what's your girlfriend do?"

"Uhm, my girlfriend? She works in Baltimore."

"Oh. Doing what?"

"In an office."

"Oh."

They got closer to the fence. Pete asked, "You're divorced? Mo was saying you're divorced."

"Right. Betty and I split up two years ago."

"You still see her?"

"Who? Betty? Naw. We went our separate ways."

"You have any kids?"

"Nope."

Of course not. When you had kids you had to think about somebody else. You couldn't think about yourself all the time.

Like Doug did.

Like Mo.

Pete was looking around again.

For squirrels, for rabbits, for witnesses.

Then Doug stopped and he looked around too. Pete wondered why, but then Doug took a bottle of beer from his knapsack and drank the whole bottle down and tossed it on the ground. "You want something to drink?" Doug asked.

"No," Pete answered. It was good that Doug'd be slightly drunk when they found him. They'd check his blood. They did that. That's how they knew Hank'd been drinking when they got the body to the Colorado Springs hospital—they checked the alcohol in the blood.

The fence was only twenty feet away.

"Oh, hey," Pete said. "Over there. Look."

He pointed to the grass on the other side of the fence.

"What?" Doug asked.

"I saw a couple of rabbits."

"You did? Where?"

"I'll show you. Come on."

"Okay. Let's do it," Doug said.

They walked to the fence. Suddenly Doug reached out and took Pete's rifle. "I'll hold it while you climb over. Safer that way."

Jesus ... Pete froze with terror. Doug was going to do exactly what Pete had thought of. He'd been planning on going to hold Doug's gun for him. And then when Doug was at the top of the fence he was going to shoot him. Making it look like Doug had tried to carry his gun as he climbed the fence but had dropped it and it went off.

Roy bet on the old law enforcement rule that what looks like an accident probably is an accident.

Pete didn't move. He thought he saw something funny in Doug's eyes, something mean and sarcastic. It reminded him of Mo's expression. Pete took one look at those eyes and could see how much Doug hated him and how much he loved Mo.

"You want me to go first?" Pete asked. Not moving, wondering if he should just run.

"Sure," Doug said. "You go first. Then I'll hand the guns over to you." His eyes said, You're not afraid of climbing over the fence, are you? You're not afraid to turn your back on me, are you?

Then Doug was looking around too.

Looking for witnesses.

"Go on," Doug encouraged.

Pete—his hands shaking now from fear, not anger—started to climb. Thinking: This is it. He's going to shoot me. I left the motel too early! Doug and Mo had kept talking and planned out how he was going to ask me down here and pretend to be all nice then he'd shoot me.

Remembering it was Doug who suggested hunting.

But if I run, Pete thought, he'll chase me down and shoot me. Even if he shoots me in the back he'll just claim it was an accident.

Roy's lawyer argued to the jury that, yes, the men had met on the path and struggled, but Hank had fallen accidentally. He urged the jury that, at worst, Roy was guilty of negligent homicide.

He put his foot on the first rung of wire. Started up.

Second rung of wire …

Pete's heart was beating a million times a minute. He had to pause to wipe his palms.

He thought he heard a whisper, as if Doug were talking to himself.

He swung his leg over the top wire.

Then he heard the sound of a gun cocking.

And Doug said in a hoarse whisper, "You're dead."

Pete gasped.

Crack!

The short, snappy sound of the .22 filled the field.

Pete choked back a cry and looked around, nearly falling off the fence.

"Damn," Doug muttered. He was aiming away from the fence. Nodding toward a tree line. "Squirrel. Missed him by two inches."

"Squirrel," Pete repeated manically. "And you missed him."

"Two goddamn inches."

Hands shaking, Pete continued over the fence and climbed to the ground.

"You okay?" Doug asked. "You look a little funny."

"I'm fine," he said.

Fine, fine, fine …

Doug handed Pete the guns and started over the fence. Pete debated. Then he put his rifle on the ground and gripped Doug's gun tight. He walked to the fence so that he was right below Doug.

"Look," Doug said as he got to the top. He was straddling it, his right leg on one side of the fence, his left on the other. "Over there." He pointed nearby.

There was a big grey lop-eared rabbit on his haunches only twenty feet away.

"There you go!" Doug whispered. "You've got a great shot."

Pete shouldered the gun. It was pointing at the ground, halfway between the rabbit and Doug.

"Go ahead. What're you waiting for?"

Roy was convicted of premeditated murder in the first degree and sentenced to life in prison. Yet he came very close to committing the perfect murder. If not for a simple twist of fate he would have gotten away with it.

Pete looked at the rabbit, looked at Doug.

"Aren't you going to shoot?"

Uhm, okay, he thought.

Pete raised the gun and pulled the trigger once.

Doug gasped, pressed at the tiny bullet hole in his chest. "But …
But … No!"

He fell backwards off the fence and lay on a patch of dried mud,
completely still. The rabbit bounded through the grass, panicked by
the sound of the shot, and disappeared in a tangle of bushes that Pete
recognized as blackberries. Mo had planted tons of them in their
backyard.

THE PLANE DESCENDED from cruising altitude and slowly floated
toward the airport.

Pete watched the billowy clouds, tried to figure out what they looked
like. He was bored. He didn't have anything to read. Before he'd talked
to the Maryland state troopers about Doug's death he'd thrown the true
crime book about the Triangle murder into a trash bin.

*One of the reasons the jury convicted Roy was that, upon examining
his house, the police found several books about disposing of evidence. Roy
had no satisfactory explanation for them.*

The small plane glided out of the skies and landed at White Plains
airport. Pete pulled his knapsack out from underneath the seat in
front of him and climbed out of the plane. He walked down the
ramp, beside the flight attendant, a tall black woman. They'd talked
together for most of the flight.

Pete saw Mo at the gate. She looked numb. She wore sunglasses
and Pete supposed she'd been crying. She was clutching a Kleenex in
her fingers.

Her nails weren't bright red anymore, he noticed.

They weren't peach either.

They were just plain fingernail colour.

The flight attendant came up to Mo. "You're Mrs. Jill Anderson?"

Mo nodded.

The woman held up a sheet of paper. "Here. Could you sign this
please?"

Numbly Mo took the pen the woman offered and signed the paper.

It was an unaccompanied-minor form, which adults had to sign to allow their children to get on planes by themselves. The parent picking up the child also had to sign it. After his parents were divorced Pete flew back and forth between Wisconsin and White Plains so often he knew all about airlines procedures for kids who flew alone.

"I have to say," she said to Mo, smiling down at Pete, "he's the best behaved youngster I've ever had on one of my flights. How old are you, Pete?"

"I'm ten," he answered. "But I'm going to be eleven next week."

She squeezed his shoulder. Then looked at Mo. "I'm so sorry about what happened," she said in a soft voice. "The trooper who put Pete on the plane told me. Your boyfriend was killed in a hunting accident?"

"No," Mo said, struggling to say the words, "he wasn't my boyfriend."

Though Pete was thinking: Of course he was your boyfriend. Except you didn't want the court to find that out because then Dad wouldn't have to pay you alimony anymore. Which is why she and Doug had been working so hard to convince Pete that Doug was "just a friend."

Can't I have friends? Aren't I allowed?

No, you're not, Pete thought. You're not going to get away with dumping me the way you dumped Dad.

"Can we go home, Mo?" he asked, looking as sad as he could. "I feel real funny about what happened."

"Sure, honey."

"Mo?" the flight attendant asked.

Mo, staring out the window, said, "When he was five Pete tried to write 'mother' on my birthday card. He just wrote M-O and didn't know how to spell the rest. It became my nickname."

"What a sweet story," the woman said and looked like *she* was going to cry. "Pete, you come back and fly with us real soon."

"Okay."

"Hey, what're you going to do for your birthday?"

"I don't know," he said. Then he looked up at his mother. "I was thinking about maybe going hiking. In Colorado. Just the two of us."

A Lifetime Burning in a Moment

by

RICK MOFINA

JOHN DEVLIN KNEW that the boys who lived in the clapboard houses by the railroad tracks not only liked beating him up, but needed to beat him up.

He was the only part of their lives they could defeat because he didn't dare hit them. Not like their fathers, who were always reeking of beer and cigarettes, or bruised mothers drowning in guilt.

"We can do whatever we want to you." The biggest boy with the broken tooth would punch Devlin's face and stomach, always failing to make him cry. "Nobody's ever going to stop us."

It was understandable then that years later colleagues at his firm would tell you that Dev, the quiet son of a widowed math teacher, listened more than he talked, as if conversation were a form of confrontation, something he had averted since the dark days of his boyhood by the railroad tracks.

As an actuary Devlin took comfort in the parameters, calculations and sums of an orderly world where everything added up. But whenever life required him to deal with mundane matters, he felt out of place. Like today, with Blake, his little boy, waiting with him in the checkout line at the auto parts store.

The air smelled of rubber, echoed with compressors and the clank of steel tools dropped in the repair bays. This was a domain of greased-stained knuckles, rolled shirt sleeves and tattooed arms; of two-day growths, ballcaps and T-shirts emblazoned with skulls, flames and creeds on living, dying.

Devlin had come to buy a pea-sized bulb for his Ford's dome light.

In line ahead of them a boy, a stranger slightly taller than Blake, turned and eyeballed Blake from head to toe. The boy's face oozed contempt before he drove his fist into Blake's shoulder. Blake tensed then retaliated with a punch just as the bigger boy's father turned to see it. The man fired glances at Blake and Devlin then drew himself to his full height. He had a scar on his chin and a toothpick in the corner of his mouth.

"What the hell're you doin'?"

Alarm rang in Devlin's ears.

"Nothing," he said. "I mean, it was a mistake. Blake, apologize."

"But Dad?" Blake's face reddened.

"We're sorry. Blake, say you're sorry."

"But he started it."

"Did not!" the bigger boy said.

"Liar!" Blake said.

"All right. Okay," Devlin laughed nervously. "Just a little harmless horseplay. We're terribly sorry."

At that, the other man's height appeared to increase as he assessed Devlin. The stranger shifted his toothpick, sucked air through his teeth then reduced Devlin to a waste of his time and turned away.

In the car, Devlin smarted from the incident but tried to conceal it as he struggled to replace the tiny bulb in the parking lot. He exaggerated his concentration, giving significance to an insignificant task. His sweating fingers lost their grip and he lost the bulb under his seat.

"Can we just go, Dad?" Blake asked.

Driving home, Devlin found his son's face in the rear view mirror and the sting of shame for having let him down.

"You have to understand something, son."

Blake watched strip malls roll by.

"Non-violence is the best way to handle these situations."

Blake said nothing.

"It's just wise to back off. Because you never know how these things are going to go. You just never—"

"It's all right, Dad."

And with those words and with his tone, Devlin's nine-year-old boy had passed judgment on him. Devlin was guilty of a monumental failing. He had been tested and shown to be a father incapable of defending his son.

At dinner that evening, Blake never revealed to his mother and his older sister what had happened. Neither did Devlin. It was not mentioned in the morning when they packed their Ford before setting off for their family vacation to the lake in eastern New Brunswick.

But it was all Devlin could think about.

It weighed on him as they drove through the rolling hills and low rugged highlands that straddled the border with Maine. They dropped the windows and cracked the sunroof. Elise, his wife, was barefoot, wearing shorts, a summer top and sunglasses. Her hair flowed in the breezes. Annie, their daughter, was listening to CDs and snapping through *Wired* magazine. Blake took in the countryside, blinking thoughtfully at the forests.

Watching him, it dawned on Devlin that Blake's reaction to the kid in the store was heroic. That in a split second he'd made a clear, morally justified choice to defend himself. Something he'd lacked the courage to do. But Blake was a boy, hardly mature enough to fathom the consequences, or appreciate the ramifications of a conflict. At least that's how Devlin tried to rationalize it as the miles passed.

They navigated the route to their rented cabin from the crudely sketched map the manager had faxed. After they got off the highway, Elise identified the landmarks. "There's the red-roofed barn, turn left there." They drove along a ribbon of pavement that wound through rolling fields and pastures creased by streams with railroad tie bridges.

It wasn't long before it narrowed into a twisting hilly dirt road, darkened by the thick cool sweet-smelling forests of cedar, pine, hemlock, butternut, maple, tamarack and birch. Under a quilt of light and shadow, the trees hid sudden peaks and valleys that hugged small cliff edges. It was beautiful, Devlin thought, loving the winding, undulating road. Annie and Blake were awed, as if they were penetrating a lost world. True to the map, after some forty-five minutes they arrived at a hamlet made up of a few buildings clustered around a sleepy four-corner stop with a blinking yellow light.

THE CROSSROADS, the hand-painted sign read.

It had a small mall with a restaurant, a postal outlet, a one-pump gas station, and Pride's General Store with a fat drowsy dog nearly asleep on its front porch.

"Pride's. That's where we pick up the key to our cabin," Elise said.

"Place looks like a ghost town." Devlin parked.

The planks of the porch creaked and the dog raised its eyebrows to greet them as they entered. Elise bought a few groceries and snacks while Devlin showed the teenage clerk his driver's licence. She produced a small envelope from the till. It contained a single bronze key with "Number 7" carved into it.

Back in the car, as they started off on the final portion of their trip, Elise tilted an open bag of potato chips to Devlin then pointed to the restaurant. "It looks nice. Let's go there for dinner after we settle in at the cabin."

"Sounds good."

The last stretch lasted some twenty minutes along a treacherous pathway that seemed even more primeval than the road they'd already travelled. Leafy branches slapped and scraped the Ford as gravel popcorned against the undercarriage. Soon the lake made its first appearance on the left, flashing between the trees in patches of brilliant blue.

It seemed so near.

"This is so cool." Annie slid off her headset. "It's like the loneliest place in the world. Like we travelled back in time or landed on a strange planet or something. I love it. It's so cool."

Blake wondered about Native legends and lost-trapper ghost stories.

"Oh, turn here." Elise pointed to a broken birch which suggested the letter T. "This is it."

Devlin stopped; dust clouds enveloped them as he inched off the road onto an earthen path curtained with a tangle of tall shrubs that swallowed their car. Through the stands of trees they glimpsed the lake and their cabin.

It was built with hand-hewn pine and had a wide deck with Adirondack chairs. There was a hammock tied between a pair of tall cedars. The cabin's lakefront wall was a floor-to-ceiling window with French doors. Inside, hardwood floors gleamed to the fieldstone fireplace.

The main floor had a large living room and dining area. The kitchen had a small fridge, freezer and stove, which were state-of-the-art energy-efficient, powered by batteries and solar panels on an exposed hillside. The sink had a pump to draw clean well water. There was a small hot water reservoir. There was a master bedroom downstairs and two large, spacious bedroom areas in the loft, which Blake and Annie found immediately.

There was one sink in the small bathroom but that was it. Beyond that there was no indoor plumbing. No toilet. No tub or shower. There was a small outhouse at the rear. The lake was where people bathed. No phone, no electricity. No computers, no Internet, no faxes. Neighbours were rare in these parts. "It's just you, the lake and the woods." Elise smiled after she'd finished reading the manager's note.

Energized, they unpacked, changed then waded into the water of their private beach to swim off the sweat and dust of the drive. Curious, Devlin walked through waist-high water to inspect the gleaming boat tied to the dock. It came with the cabin.

"Think you can drive it?" Elise smiled.

"You bet, let's go for a ride."

They all climbed into the aluminum craft. The 25-horsepower outboard came to life with a bubbling rumble that churned a creamy white wake as Devlin eased it ahead before opening up the throttle. The motor whined, raising the bow as he adjusted the tiller, centring its point squarely on the middle of the lake. Warm breezes brushed their faces.

It felt good.

A baptism of sorts, Devlin thought, warmed by the absence of others.

Bedrock as old as time formed the distant peaks that guarded the lake. They jutted from rolling forests laced with clear-water streams and meadows jewelled with red trilliums, orange daylilies, blue flags, and bunchberries. The lake was known as God's secret sanctuary, according to the history Devlin had read. For years, it was all but forgotten, hidden in a remote reach of Canada's border with New England. Other than an abandoned Jesuit outpost, no lasting settlements had ever been recorded here. Much of the territory had remained unexplored well into the late 1800s. The demanding terrain had repelled lumber companies.

In 1893, a Halifax shipping tycoon bought a four hundred–acre section surrounding the lake. He died without ever having set foot on it. His acquisition was ignored by his estate, except for the sale of a few lakeside tracts to satisfy an obscure turn-of-the-century property requirement. Situated on a peninsula, the parcels were separated by several acres of dense forest and accessed by narrow bush roads. It resembled skeletal fingers shaping a claw, the final extension of some unfortunate who had reached the lake to die.

"See." Devlin pointed his fork at the map on the paper placemats in the restaurant, where later that day, after the boat ride, he continued telling his family about the region's history over a dinner.

"Like a skeleton's hand," Blake agreed. "Mom, where's our map, so we can see where our cabin is and where we drove in the boat?"

"In the car on the front dash. We'll check later, sweetie."

Devlin and his wife had club sandwiches. The kids had cheeseburgers. They were the only customers. After dessert of homemade apple pie and ice cream, they strolled outside for some window shopping at the adjacent craft shop which had just closed for the day.

"This place is a dead zone," Annie said after oohing and ahhing with her mother over a bracelet in the shop window. As they turned to leave, Devlin saw a man walking away quickly from the side of their Ford to a pickup truck in a far corner of the empty lot.

He'd thought nothing of it until his family approached their doors and Devlin saw the beer bottle wedged between the right rear tire and the ground.

He stared.

It had been placed strategically so it would shatter and shred their tire when they drove off. Now why would someone do something like that? Devlin glanced around for an answer, glimpsing the man nearing the pickup. He heard the man's snickering, echoing with the chuckling of a second man waiting behind the wheel of the truck.

For a few heated seconds Devlin didn't move. The sight of the bottle hit him. The laughter hit him. Like blows to his stomach, his head, his dignity, they pounded him back through time, past the humiliation in the auto shop, back through his life to the railyard beatings. He began walking to the truck without realizing he was heading that way until Elise begged him to come back.

Devlin kept walking.

It might've been because all his life he'd failed to stand up for himself. Had always bit back on his anger. It might've been because he'd failed to stand up for Blake. It might've been the pressure pent up from years of never standing up to anyone. But deep in his gut, Devlin felt the quaking of an explosion. You just don't pull a stunt like this, laugh and walk away. No sir. There had to be an accounting. And by God, he'd eaten too much crap in his life not to be entitled to a little respect. Indignation hammered in his chest as he neared the truck.

The engine started.

The battered truck lumbered triumphantly toward the lot's exit, ticking and creaking. As it moved away slowly, the two men looked at Devlin. He stared into the darkened cab then glanced at his family, feeling their fear pulling him back to the safety of doing nothing. To let it go. But he couldn't let it go.

Something was burning with such intensity it consumed him.

A sudden yelp of laughter triggered his final decision.

Devlin trotted after the pickup. Planting himself alone in the lot, he pulled out his weapons. A pen and notebook. Defiantly ignoring the fact that the two men were watching him in their mirrors, he scrawled down their plate.

Good. He had their number. That's all he needed, he thought, turning to join his family in their car.

"John, what's wrong with you?" his wife asked. "Running after those two guys. That was so foolish."

"Excuse me," Blake said.

"Yeah, Dad!" Annie said. "It was so embarrassing!"

"Excuse me," Blake said.

"Why didn't you just let it go?" his wife said.

"Excuse me," Blake said. "But I think those guys are coming over here."

The truck had veered from its course and was approaching them. Devlin's Adam's apple lifted then dropped. He hadn't expected this.

"Please just stay in the car," his wife said. "Calm down and don't make this any worse. Kids, put your windows up."

Devlin pressed the button automatically locking all four doors. The truck ticked and creaked as it eased beside him, stopping when the driver's door drew up across from Devlin's, leaving about six feet between them. The driver's window was down. Devlin lowered his.

Halfway.

One muscular arm tattooed with a spider's web was draped over the truck's wheel, the other rested on the door frame. The old pickup had a beat-up fibreglass cap over the bed and a crumpled front fender, as if it'd rammed something. The driver took his time dragging on his cigarette and spewing a smoke stream to the sky before turning to Devlin.

"Is there a problem, mister?"

Devlin figured the man to be his age. He was wearing dark glasses, a filthy ballcap and looked as though he hadn't shaved for several days.

"Your friend seems to have misplaced his beer bottle under my tire. I think he wanted to give me a flat."

"Give you a flat?"

The man's face soured. He turned to his passenger who appeared mystified. The driver turned back to Devlin.

"I think you're mistaken."

"Mistaken?" Devlin made a point of surveying the empty lot. "You're right. Obviously, with no one else here, it couldn't have been you."

The air tightened as if a gun had been cocked.

"John, please!" his wife whispered.

"John?" The man had heard. "That your name?"

The driver said something to his passenger and they laughed. Devlin couldn't make out what he'd said about his name as Elise squeezed his knee. He glanced at the frightened faces of his children in the mirror. Elise was now squeezing so hard it hurt.

"I'm sorry," Devlin said. "It was a bad joke. You're right. I'm mistaken. It must've rolled under there. I'm sorry I chased you. I was wrong. Please forget it."

"Did you call me a bad joke, John?"

Devlin saw his reflection in the driver's dark glasses. Tiny. Small, shrinking away, as he always did.

"No. Forgive me. I made a bad joke. I was wrong to accuse you of anything. Totally out of line. I apologize."

The driver's face hardened as he and his passenger scanned Devlin, his family and their car for a long, cold moment. Then the driver studied his cigarette butt. Before he flicked it away, he half grinned and nodded.

"No harm done, John."

The truck's motor ticked as it rolled away then vanished down the road.

Elise wanted them to wait. So they did. For a long moment, Devlin sat motionless behind the wheel. Then he cursed under his breath, turned the Ford's ignition and started back to their cabin along the serpentine dirt road.

No one spoke.

The ping of gravel punctuated the silence, decompressing the tension as each of them withdrew into their thoughts. Devlin soon took comfort in the soft strains of music leaking from Annie's headset as she listened to a CD. Blake looked toward the lake while Elise glimpsed at her passenger side mirror.

"Oh God, they're following us!"

Devlin's skin prickled when he saw the pickup's grill and damaged front fender half-concealed like a phantom in the dust behind them.

"Hang on!"

He accelerated and the Ford roared along the narrow route, bobbing on its sudden hills and valleys, sunlight flashing through the thick woods, branches slapping the car as stones boiled against its undercarriage.

"Daddee!" Annie gripped her armrest.

Blake was numb with fear.

"Oh God, John," his wife said.

"We just need to buy some distance." Devlin's ears pounded with each curve he rounded. "There it is." He braked, the car slid, creating thick, choking dust clouds as he turned into the underbrush of their entrance. The Ford bounced. He tucked it neatly into a leafy canopy and shut off the motor.

No one moved.

For several desperate moments they heard nothing but their breathing, which halted when the pickup approached—crunching gravel then the ticking engine. Under her breath Elise prayed for the two strangers to please just go away. Seconds later the truck rolled through their fading dust curtain, leaving another in its wake.

Devlin allowed a full minute to pass before he turned to Elise.

"Well that was an adventure," he smiled weakly. "All right back there?"

"Just fine, Dad," Annie groaned.

Elise shook her head, muttering something about brainless men.

"I think that's the end of it," Devlin said. "I think it's over."

That night they built a fire by the beach, huddled together, toasted marshmallows and watched the constellations wheel by as Devlin assured Blake and Annie that everything was fine. Later, after the children had gone to bed, Devlin and Elise lay awake and considered telling the police about what had happened. But Devlin hesitated.

"When you think about it, it was really nothing."

"John, what if those men come to our cabin?"

"El, those idiots were drinking, probably passing through town and decided to have fun at our expense."

"I hope you're right."

"Sure I'm right. They're probably passed out, or a hundred miles away by now."

That's what Devlin wanted to believe as he stared into the darkness, listening to every sound in the night until finally he was taken by sleep. It was accompanied by a dream that Elise was shaking him and wouldn't stop until he— "John, wake up. There's something outside!"

"Wha-what?"

At that moment, there was a wooden snap near their window. Oh Christ, Devlin thought, swallowing hard. Then all went quiet.

"I'm scared, John do something!"

Quickly and quietly Devlin pulled on his jeans, found the new flashlight he'd bought specially for the trip and crept to the deck for the axe he used for the fire. He padded around the cabin in the pitch black in time to hear a rustling in the bush near the bedroom window. His flashlight beam captured the furry fat behind and striped tail of a raccoon vanishing into the forest.

When he told Elise they had to stifle their laughter.

"This is just too silly," she said before falling soundly to sleep.

The next morning was glorious.

Devlin spent much of it reading *Crime and Punishment* in the hammock. Elise and Annie collected wildflowers in front of the cabin while Blake fished off the dock. For lunch, they cooked hotdogs over an open fire near the beach. That afternoon, when Devlin went to the car for his copy of *Ulysses,* he noticed the Ford was leaning at an odd angle. Then he discovered why. The right rear tire was flat.

The same tire that those jerks had targeted.

And there was another problem, but before Devlin could figure out a way to deal with it, Elise was standing behind him, hands thrust to her face.

"It was them," she said. "Those two assholes did it in the night." Elise never swore. She turned to look at Blake and Annie on the dock. "I want to go home."

Devlin tried to calm her by pointing to a rusted nail.

"It wasn't them. Look, this is why the tire's flat," he told her. "We simply ran over a nail. The bad news is we don't have a spare. No jack, nothing. We pulled it all out to pack more stuff in the trunk. It was dumb."

"My God, John what are we going to do?"

Devlin had an idea and told her. They all climbed into their boat. The outboard rumbled as they cut across the water under a darkening sky. Taking stock of the forested hills and the vast lake, Devlin felt imprisoned and vulnerable but kept his thoughts to himself.

They had no other option.

It was a long time before they reached the Crossroads and the gas station where Devlin asked the attendant to send someone out to fix his tire.

"That's going to take a couple of days. Jed's got the truck and he went to the city. His wife's having a baby. Besides he's going to have to pick you up a new tire, too. We don't have much stock here. I'd say, day after tomorrow is the soonest."

Devlin saw worry creep into Elise's face.

"Is there anyone else, or a spare, anything?"

The attendant shook his head. Devlin squeezed her hand.

"We'll be fine."

They returned to their cabin and finished their vacation without a single incident. Not even a chipmunk to startle them in the night. Relief came two days later when Jed, a twenty-something under-the-hood type, with a nice smile, arrived to fix their tire. It was perfect timing. While he worked, the Devlins packed. When he finished, Jed showed off pictures of his baby daughter.

"She's brand new," he beamed as Elise cooed. "We named her Ivy. She's the good news that we need in the county, especially after what happened a few days back at the north end of the lake."

Elise and Devlin looked at each other then stared at Jed.

"What're you talking about?"

"That's right, you wouldn't know—being out here all isolated and stranded with your tire situation." Jed went to the cab of his truck, came back and handed Devlin a newspaper, *The County Beacon.* The main story on the front page was headlined:

"Triple Murder: Retired Doctor, Wife, Grandson, Slain At Cabin"

Devlin and Elise read how police suspected the killers had followed the doctor and his family to their remote lake property in what one source called a gruesome multiple homicide. "In all my years I've never seen anything like this."

Devlin's heart leapt when he read the next paragraphs. Investigators were seeking the public's help locating a vehicle seen in the area at the time. "A dark, older model pickup truck with a damaged front fender and a light-coloured cap over the bed. Two male occupants were seen inside."

When they finished packing, John Devlin and his family drove for three hours to the RCMP subdivision.

Sergeant Lew Segretti of the Major Crimes Section was one of the Mounties investigating the killings. He took careful notes. Another member brought coffee, juice and doughnuts for the kids.

"Your encounter with the men in the pickup, your description of the tattoo, could be a critical lead. We'll keep you posted," Segretti told Devlin.

They returned to the city and the routine of their quiet lives, trying and failing to put the incident behind them. Devlin scrutinized the newspapers and TV reports, but the story faded. Weeks passed, a month, then three until one weekend afternoon when Devlin got a call at home during the first quarter of the football game.

"Is this Mr. John Devlin?"

"Yes it is."

"Lew Segretti, RCMP Major Crimes. You provided us information on the Cushing family murders at the lake?"

"Yes, Sergeant."

"Mr. Devlin, there's been a break in the case, and it stems from your report. It led us to two suspects, Aaron Sikes and Daniel Johnson. Both dead now."

"Dead?"

"They tried shooting it out with the ERT team in a trailer in the foothills near Pincher Creek."

Devlin's pulse quickened.

"Mr. Devlin, we couldn't tell you at the time, but your thorough description was the linchpin. It helped us identify them. Sikes and Johnson were a murder team. We've connected them to the three homicides here and four in Ontario. We've been working with police across Canada, tracking these men until they led us to K-Division."

"I'm sorry?"

"Alberta."

"Alberta. I see, and you're certain both are dead?" Devlin said.

"One hundred per cent. Johnson died at the scene. Sikes died in Lethbridge a few hours later."

"In hospital?"

"Yes, but before Sikes died, sir, he spoke to one of our members, who took a declaration, a taped final statement. I think you'd better sit down. I have a transcript and he mentions your encounter."

Devlin cast about the room. His wife was in the doorway holding a dish towel. Devlin swallowed.

"I'll just summarize it, but Sikes told the Corporal that he and Johnson had selected you and your family."

"Selected? Selected for what?"

Segretti hesitated. "To kill you." The hairs on the back of Devlin's neck stood up as the Mountie continued. "But you'd spotted the bottle, confronted them and somehow threw them off their game. That's why they pursued the older couple, Doctor Cushing, which is horrible and our sympathies go to the Cushing family. But the point is, your action saved not only the lives of your family, but of seven more people."

"I don't understand."

"Mr. Devlin, these men were psychopaths. They were not very sophisticated, not clever the way the movies make out. But they were extremely dangerous. They had targeted another family in Alberta, a single mother who lived with her six kids on a rural property in an isolated area near the Rockies around Pincher Creek and Cardston. They were about to move on her and her children when we locked on to them, because of what you did. You stopped them. We just wanted you to know that, sir."

Segretti ended the call, but Devlin sat dumbfounded with the phone in his hand for the longest time.

"John, was that the RCMP?"

"Yes, they got the guys. They're dead. It's over."

"Did they tell you everything?"

Devlin nodded and his mind reeled, racing at the speed of memory back through the stand-off at the Crossroads, back through his humiliation at the auto parts store, back to his youth and the beatings he took from other boys at the railyard.

The boys who'd said he would never stop them.

The Visitors' Book

by

SOPHIE HANNAH

I AM NOT A SNOB. My parents are snobs—every member of my family apart from me is a snob—and I am nothing like any of them. I do not, as my sister Lydia does, own a black cat with one paw that's white that I've named "Paw White Trash," "Trash" for short. My mother commits the details of the *Sunday Times* Rich List to memory; I don't. Alex is the snob, not me. At the very least, he's a pretentious idiot.

He's standing with his back to me, opening a bottle of wine. I shouldn't say anything. I should let it go. Except that, after what I've just discovered about him, I want to have the row more than I want Alex as a boyfriend. "I'm not a snob," I say.

When we got out of the cab and I first saw his house, my reaction was entirely neutral. It was just a house. It only occurred to me in the light of what happened next that Alex's home is a two-up two-down back-to-back terrace on a street lined with similar houses, red-brick on one side, white-rendering-dirtied-to-grey on the other. Alex's is one of the red bricks.

What else did I notice? Washing hanging on lines in small square front yards, net curtains to ward off nosey passersby. Some clean cars, some dirty; one half collapsed, missing its front two wheels. I didn't see Alex's house and think, "Oh dear, it's not a detached mansion"— why would I? I live in a tiny two-bedroom flat above a jeweller's shop.

"A snob is my least favourite sort of person," Alex says matter-of-factly, as if he might not be talking about me.

"I'm *not* a snob," I insist.

"When I asked you to sign the Visitors' Book, you laughed as if it was the most hilarious thing in the world." He smiles and hands me a glass of wine. "Tell me what you found so funny, and we'll see if there's an element of snobbery involved." He doesn't sound angry, or offended. He sounds ... analytical is the only way I can describe it, as if he's interested intellectually, but it doesn't matter to him. It makes me feel uneasy.

I stare down at the large green leather-bound book that's spread open in front of me on the kitchen table. The Visitors' Book: that's what he called it and that's what it appears to be. It has the words "Visitors' Book" on the cover in gold cursive writing. I flick through the pages, skimming the comments: "Netterden is a fantastic house! We shall remember our visit with great fondness—The Flemings"; "We had such fun and will take away with us plenty of memories to treasure—Winnifred and John Santandreu, Islington, London"; "The views from the terrace at dusk are breathtaking—Richard and Sue Graham." Different inks, different handwritings—most are shaky and erratic, as if the writers were sloshed, or too old and doddery to care. The book appears to be genuine. How utterly preposterous.

"You're telling me no one else has laughed at this?" I say, wondering if I'm the only non-pretentious person in Alex's social circle.

"Have you never signed a visitors' book before?" he asks.

"Yes, plenty. Some friends and I hired a Manor House in Devon once, to celebrate finishing our degrees. Wortham Manor—it was several hundred years old ..."

"Exactly the sort of place where you'd expect to find a visitors' book," Alex cuts me off.

"I also ..." I stop, realizing that what I'm about to say might be taken as further evidence of my snobbishness.

"Go on."

"My godmother is married to a Lord—you know, in the House of Lords."

"I didn't think you meant a Lord in the heavens above," says Alex. His sense of humour was what first attracted me to him.

"They've got a Visitors' Book in their Hampshire mansion."

"Which you signed without laughing?"

"Credit me with some manners," I say impatiently.

"Yet you laughed at me," Alex observes—again, apparently without feeling. Why do I find it so unsettling, his unwillingness to take this personally?

"Alex, you don't live in a mansion, or a historical manor house. Those are the sorts of houses that have visitors' books. Your house just ... *isn't*. Look, is this a prank? Did you forge all these different handwritings yourself? This is too ridiculous—I can't take it seriously."

"You think I've got ideas above my station," says Alex. "You're wrong."

"It's not about above or below. It's ..." He must be able to see it. Until five minutes ago, I thought he was sane and normal. "It's about *context*. If I saw Prince Charles walking down the road wearing a Babygro, I'd laugh. Whereas I wouldn't laugh if I saw a *baby* wearing a Babygro! I don't think Prince Charles is worse, or less deserving of a Babygro than a baby is. I'd laugh because it's a weird and surprising context in which to see a Babygro, just as a two-bedroom terraced house belonging to a twenty-nine-year-old inner-city-secondary-school history teacher is an unusual context for a visitors' book!"

"Mightn't a history teacher want to keep a record of the people who visit his home, for sentimental reasons?" Alex asks, sipping his wine. "Think about it: history."

It's the first good point he's made. For a second, I wonder if he's sensible and open-minded and I'm a bigoted fool. Then I come to my senses. "Netterden," I snap. "One of those comments referred to the house as Netterden. Whereas your front door seems to think it's called number thirty-two."

"So it's pretentious to give a house a name? This from the woman who buys a car with a number plate that ends LMO and immediately christens it Elmo."

"That's different," I protest. Why do I feel as if he's winning?

"I bet your godmother's Hampshire mansion has a name, doesn't it? And you don't think there's anything wrong with that."

"My godmother's house *needs* a name, for the simple reason that it isn't on a street. They could hardly call it 27, The Middle of a Load of Greenery, could they?"

"You can think of no hypothesis that would allow me to have a visitors' book in my house and *not* be absurdly pretentious? Then, like all snobs, you lack imagination."

I stand up. "I'm going," I say. "Do you want to ring for the butler, or shall I show myself out?"

"You're making a mistake," he says. His tone suggests that my error doesn't matter to him, but ought to matter to me.

I slam the front door behind me and march down the street without looking back. I have no idea where I'm going, where the nearest bus stop or tube station is. My mind is full of jagged scraps of ideas that clash into one another, random and incoherent. A quote flashes in my brain: *"Last night I dreamed I went to Manderley again."* I laugh out loud. I am *not* crazy. Daphne du Maurier, who also wasn't crazy, knew when she wrote the first line of *Rebecca* that Manderley *had* to be the name of a vast country estate. Would the novel have become a classic if Maxim de Winter had lived in a two-bed terrace in Walthamstow? No, it would not. Mrs. Danvers would have had to sleep in the second bedroom, a stone's throw from the first; she'd have heard her boss and his new wife having sex through the thin partition wall.

Netterden! Did he call it that because the street's full of scuzzy net curtains? All right, perhaps I am a snob. I don't care if I am.

Alex is the crazy one—him and all his freakish friends who wrote those pompous comments. The Flemings, Winnifred and John Santandreu, from Islington, London …

I stop walking as a chilly fear seeps through me, pinning me to the spot. *Islington, London.* Walthamstow is also in London. Why wouldn't the Santandreus simply have written "Islington"? Surely you wouldn't write "Islington, London" unless … I shiver. Unless you were writing in the visitors' book of a house that was outside London. And there's something else, something I can't put my finger on that's not quite right. It's like a shadow snagging at the back of my mind. What is it?

I turn round to check Alex isn't following me. He isn't; it's safe to stand here and allow myself to work it out. *Safe.* Since when have I been scared of him?

I try to remember other entries I read. There was one from a Richard and Sue something-or-other. Richard and Sue Graham. "The views from the terrace at dusk are breathtaking." No; it's all wrong. No one would say that about a terraced house. No one would call it "the terrace"—I am sure of this. Not Richard and Sue Graham; not anybody. They might say, "The views from the *house* at dusk are breathtaking." Except they aren't. It's round about dusk now—not quite dark yet, but not light either. Isn't that what dusk means?

Why didn't this occur to me before, when I first read those words? I was too busy skimming the pages for evidence of Alex's pretentiousness.

I must have seen the word *terrace* and thought that since Alex's house *is* a terrace …

I feel sick, shaky. I'm certain those words weren't written about the house I've just left, the view from which, at dusk or at any other time, is of a row of dirty white houses on an unremarkable—some might say shabby—street. True, I didn't look out of any of the back windows, but Alex lives in Walthamstow, for goodness' sake. How breathtaking can the view from the back bedroom possibly be? There's nothing for miles around but rows of terraced houses on treeless streets.

Richard and Sue Graham can't have been writing about Alex's home. Wherever and whatever Netterden is, it isn't a terrace; it *has* a terrace—perhaps with a stone balustrade, certainly with a fantastic view of the grounds—where people might sit and sip champagne cocktails as the sun goes down. At dusk.

Why didn't Alex tell me the truth? And if Netterden isn't his house, what's he doing with its Visitors' Book? Why did he show it to me? I close my eyes, try to picture what happened. The book was on the kitchen table when we walked in. I said, "What's this?" as I sat down. He didn't draw it to my attention—I noticed it and asked about it. *That's* what prompted him to ask if I wanted to sign it. Maybe he'd been looking at it earlier, before he came out to meet me, and, in his rush to leave the house, he forgot to put it away. He very quickly called me a snob when I laughed, before I had time to focus on how odd it was, how the comments couldn't have been referring to the house I was in. He was gambling on being able to distract me, make me focus instead on defending myself.

I still can't summon the not-quite-right detail, the snag at the back of my mind. Perhaps it will come to me. Perhaps, as what's left of the daylight disappears and dusk gives way to night, a light will come on in my brain and I'll have it.

Thinking about it, Alex never said his house was called Netterden. He was more careful, more precise. He said, "So it's pretentious to give a house a name?," and asked if I couldn't think of another hypothesis to explain his having a visitors' book.

He must have stolen it. From the real Netterden. If it was in his possession for a legitimate reason, why not say so? I shudder as my memory recreates the expression on his face as we argued, completely devoid of emotion.

How far am I from a library? I've no idea, and I'm not calm enough to set about finding out. I pull my mobile out of my bag and ring "118118." When a woman answers, I ask for Santandreu in Islington. I have to spell the name twice.

"I've got a Winnifred Santandreu on Gladsmuir Road, Islington," says the woman. It must be her. How many Winnifred Santandreus can there be in London? I ask to be connected. A few seconds later, a man's voice says, "Hello, Michael Santandreu speaking."

"May I speak to Winnifred?" I ask. "Or John?"

"My parents passed on in January 2006," he says abruptly. "Who are you? Not a friend or former colleague, if you didn't know."

"My name's Francesca Woodham-Blake. Look, I'm sorry, I'll leave you alone. It's not important." They *both* died in January 2006? I can't decide if it's odd. Perhaps I'm the odd one, and the rest of the world is normal.

"What did you want?" asks Michael Santandreu.

"It's not important." Why did I say that? It *is* important—it's the most important thing in my world at the moment.

"I might be able to help you with whatever it is," he insists, determined to make me declare my business.

"I was going to ask them if they remembered visiting a house called Netterden, but, as I said, it's really not …"

"Netterden." He throws the word at me like a stone.

"What?" I ask, startled.

There's a long pause, as if he's debating whether or not to tell me. "That's where my parents were when they died," he says eventually.

"Pardon?" I manage to say. The world tips on its axis.

"It's one of Gloucestershire's oldest houses. I think the Landmark Trust owns it now. It used to belong to Penny and Clive Hoddy. That's where my parents died—at one of Penny and Clive's parties. Look, if you don't know what happened in January 2006, why are you asking about Netterden?"

Alex's surname is Penny. His middle name is Clive. I teased him about it on our first date. I hold on to a wall to steady myself.

"Please, just … tell me," I say faintly. "I can explain why I want to know." But don't ask me to explain now, I silently plead with him. Hear the desperation in my voice and understand that I need to know, straight away.

"Twenty-three people died that night—everybody there. My aunt and uncle too—Sarah and Peter Fleming."

The Flemings. I know without needing to be told that Richard and Sue Graham are also dead. There were no dates in the Visitors' Book. None. *That's* the detail that was bothering me, the one I couldn't call to mind. People who sign visitors' books always write the date. *Unless they're doing it at gunpoint, all on the same day—their last day. What does the date matter if you're about to die?* I think about the shaky handwriting, and about how terror would make a person's hand shake more than alcohol or old age. But the comments they wrote … were they forced to come up with the wording themselves? Did they have their entries dictated to them? I can't bear to think about it.

"You haven't …" Michael Santandreu clears his throat. "You didn't hear about it, on the news?"

I don't watch the news, or read the papers. "What happened?" I ask. It's all I can do to hold myself upright.

"Somebody, or should I say two people, shot them all—all the guests, Penny and Clive, their daughter Eleanor. I'm sorry, there's no nice way of putting it. The cleaner found the … bodies the following Monday morning, purses, wallets and bags missing. Most of them had pens in their hands—I've no idea why, and the police still don't have a clue what it might mean. In a way, that remains the biggest mystery."

"Who …?" I start to ask, though I know the answer. *Two people. Who was the other one?*

"Penny and Clive's two sons were and still are the only suspects—they disappeared that night and haven't surfaced since. There was no break-in, you see."

Pens in their hands …

"Thomas and Alex," says Michael Santandreu. "I met them once or twice. There's absolutely no doubt in my mind that they did it."

There's no doubt in mine either, but in my panic I can't help saying, "It might have been anyone."

"No," says Michael. "Those two weren't right in the head. They hated their family, thought their parents were appalling snobs. No doubt they thought mine were too, and all the other guests at Netterden that night."

I hear a noise behind me. I turn, see Alex walking towards me, smiling. It is still light enough for me to see his face: still dusk. He is holding a pen in one hand, the Visitors' Book in the other.

The Poison That Leaves No Trace

by

SUE GRAFTON

THE WOMAN WAS WAITING outside my office when I arrived that morning. She was short and quite plump, wearing jeans in a size I've never seen on the rack. Her blouse was tunic-length, ostensibly to disguise her considerable rear end. Someone must have told her never to wear horizontal stripes, so the bold red-and-blue bands ran diagonally across her torso with a dizzying effect. Big red canvas tote, matching canvas wedgies. Her face was round, seamless, and smooth, her hair a uniformly dark shade that suggested a rinse. She might have been any age between forty and sixty. "You're not Kinsey Millhone," she said as I approached.

"Actually, I am. Would you like to come in?" I unlocked the door and stepped back so she could pass in front of me. She was giving me the once-over, as if my appearance was as remarkable to her as hers was to me.

She took a seat, keeping her tote squarely on her lap. I went around to my side of the desk, pausing to open the French doors before I sat down. "What can I help you with?"

She stared at me openly. "Well, I don't know. I thought you'd be a man. What kind of name is Kinsey? I never heard such a thing."

"My mother's maiden name. I take it you're in the market for a private investigator."

"I guess you could say that. I'm Shirese Dunaway, but everybody calls me Sis. Exactly how long have you been doing this?" Her tone was a perfect mating of skepticism and distrust.

"Six years in May. I was with the police department for two years before that. If my being a woman bothers you, I can recommend another agency. It won't offend me in the least."

"Well, I might as well talk to you as long as I'm here. I drove all the way up from Orange County. You don't charge for a consultation, I hope."

"Not at all. My regular fee is thirty dollars an hour plus expenses, but only if I believe I can be of help. What sort of problem are you dealing with?"

"Thirty dollars an hour! My stars. I had no idea it would cost so *much*."

"Lawyers charge a hundred and twenty," I said with a shrug.

"I know, but that's in case of a lawsuit. Contingency, or whatever they call that. Thirty dollars an *hour* ..."

I closed my mouth and let her work it out for herself. I didn't want to get into an argument with the woman in the first five minutes of our relationship. I tuned her out, watching her lips move while she decided what to do.

"The problem is my sister," she said at long last. "Here, look at this." She handed me a little clipping from the Santa Teresa newspaper.

The death notice read: "Crispin, Margery, beloved mother of Justine, passed away on December 10. Private arrangements. Wynington-Blake Mortuary."

"Nearly two months ago," I remarked.

"Nobody even told me she was sick! That's the point," Sis Dunaway snapped. "I wouldn't know to this day if a former neighbour hadn't spotted this and cut it out." She tended to speak in an indignant tone regardless of the subject.

"You just received this?"

"Well, no. It came back in January, but of course I couldn't drop everything and rush right up. This is the first chance I've had. You can probably appreciate that, upset as I was."

"Absolutely," I said. "When did you last talk to Margery?"

"I don't remember the exact date. It had to be eight or ten years back. You can imagine my shock! To get something like this out of a clear blue sky."

I shook my head. "Terrible," I murmured. "Have you talked to your niece?"

She gestured dismissively. "That Justine's a mess. Marge had her hands full with that one," she said. "I stopped over to her place and you should have seen the look I got. I said, 'Justine, whatever in the world did Margery die of?' And you know what she said? Said, 'Aunt Sis, her heart give out.' Well, I knew that was bull the minute she said it. We have never had heart trouble in our family...."

She went on for a while about what everybody'd died of; Mom, Dad, Uncle Buster, Rita Sue. We're talking cancer, lung disorders, an aneurysm or two. Sure enough, no heart trouble. I was making sympathetic noises, just to keep the tale afloat until she got to the point. I jotted down a few notes, though I never did quite understand how Rita Sue was related. Finally, I said, "Is it your feeling there was something unusual in your sister's death?"

She pursed her lips and lowered her gaze. "Let's put it this way. I can smell a rat. I'd be willing to *bet* Justine had a hand in it."

"Why would she do that?"

"Well, Marge had that big insurance policy. The one Harley took out in 1966. If that's not a motive for murder, I don't know what is." She sat back in her chair, content that she'd made her case.

"Harley?"

"Her husband ... until he passed on, of course. They took out policies on each other and after he went, she kept up the premiums on hers. Justine was made the beneficiary. Marge never remarried and with Justine on the policy, I guess she'll get all the money and do I don't know what. It just doesn't seem right. She's been a sneak all her natural life. A regular con artist. She's been in jail four times! My sister talked till she was blue in the face, but she never could get Justine to straighten up her act."

"How much money are we talking about?"

"A hundred thousand dollars," she said. "Furthermore, them two never did get along. Fought like cats and dogs since the day Justine was born. Competitive? My God. Always trying to get the better of each other. Justine as good as told me they had a falling-out not two months before her mother died! The two had not exchanged a word since the day Marge got mad and stomped off."

"They lived together?"

"Well, yes, until this big fight. Next thing you know, Marge is dead. You tell me there's not something funny going on."

"Have you talked to the police?"

"How can I do that? I don't have any *proof.*"

"What about the insurance company? Surely, if there were something irregular about Marge's death, the claims investigator would have picked up on it."

"Oh, honey, you'd think so, but you know how it is. Once a claim's been paid, the insurance company doesn't want to hear. Admit they made a mistake? Uh-uh, no thanks. Too much trouble going back through all the paperwork. Besides, Justine would probably turn around and sue 'em within an inch of their life. They'd rather turn a deaf ear and write the money off."

"When was the claim paid?"

"A week ago, they said."

I stared at her for a moment, considering. "I don't know what to tell you, Ms. Dunaway...."

"Call me Sis. I don't go for that Ms. bull."

"All right, Sis. If you're really convinced Justine's implicated in her mother's death, of course I'll try to help. I just don't want to waste your time."

"I can appreciate that," she said.

I stirred in my seat. "Look, I'll tell you what let's do. Why don't you pay me for two hours of my time. If I don't come up with anything concrete in that period, we can have another conversation and you can decide then if you want me to proceed."

"Sixty dollars," she said.

"That's right. Two hours."

"Well, all right. I guess I can do that." She opened her tote and peeled six tens off a roll of bills she'd secured with a rubber band. I wrote out an abbreviated version of a standard contract. She said she'd be staying in town overnight and gave me the telephone number at the motel where she'd checked in. She handed me the death notice. I made sure I had her sister's full name and the exact date of her death and told her I'd be in touch.

My first stop was the Hall of Records at the Santa Teresa County Courthouse two and a half blocks away. I filled out a copy order, supplying the necessary information, and paid seven bucks in cash. An hour later, I returned to pick up the certified copy of Margery Crispin's death certificate. Cause of death was listed as a "myocardial infarction." The certificate was signed by Dr. Yee, one of the contract pathologists out at the county morgue. If Marge Crispin had been the victim of foul play, it was hard to believe Dr. Yee wouldn't have spotted it.

I swung back by the office and picked up my car, driving over to Wynington-Blake, the mortuary listed in the newspaper clipping. I asked for Mr. Sharonson, whom I'd met when I was working on another case. He was wearing a sombre charcoal-grey suit, his tone of voice carefully modulated to reflect the solemnity of his work. When I mentioned Marge Crispin, a shadow crossed his face.

"You remember the woman?"

"Oh, yes," he said. He closed his mouth then, but the look he gave me was eloquent.

I wondered if funeral home employees took a loyalty oath, vowing never to divulge a single fact about the dead. I thought I'd prime the pump a bit. Men are worse gossips than women once you get 'em going. "Mrs. Crispin's sister was in my office a little while ago and she seems to think there was something … uh, irregular about the woman's death."

I could see Mr. Sharonson formulate his response. "I wouldn't say there was anything *irregular* about the woman's death, but there was certainly something sordid about the circumstances."

"Oh?" said I.

He lowered his voice, glancing around to make certain we couldn't be overheard. "The two were estranged. Hadn't spoken for months as I understand it. The woman died alone in a seedy hotel on lower State Street. She drank."

"Nooo," I said, conveying disapproval and disbelief.

"Oh, yes," he said. "The police picked up the body, but she wasn't identified for weeks. If it hadn't been for the article in the paper, her daughter might not have ever known."

"What article?"

"Oh, you know the one. There's that columnist for the local paper who does all those articles about the homeless. He did a write-up about the poor woman. 'Alone in Death' I think it was called. He talked about how pathetic this woman was. Apparently, when Ms. Crispin read the article, she began to suspect it might be her mother. That's when she went out there to take a look."

"Must have been a shock," I said. "The woman died of natural causes?"

"Oh, yes."

"No evidence of trauma, foul play, anything like that?"

"No, no, no. I tended her myself and I know they ran toxicology tests. I guess at first they thought it might be acute alcohol poisoning, but it turned out to be her heart."

I quizzed him on a number of possibilities, but I couldn't come up with anything out of the ordinary. I thanked him for his time, got back in my car, and drove over to the trailer park where Justine Crispin lived.

The trailer itself had seen better days. It was moored in a dirt patch with a wooden crate for an outside step. I knocked on the door, which opened about an inch to show a short strip of round face peering out at me. "Yes?"

"Are you Justine Crispin?"

"Yes."

"I hope I'm not bothering you. My name is Kinsey Millhone. I'm an old friend of your mother's and I just heard she passed away."

The silence was cautious. "Who'd you hear that from?"

I showed her the clipping. "Someone sent me this. I couldn't believe my eyes. I didn't even know she was sick."

Justine's eyes darkened with suspicion. "When did you see her last?"

I did my best to imitate Sis Dunaway's folksy tone. "Oh, gee. Must have been last summer. I moved away in June and it was probably some time around then because I remember giving her my address. It was awfully sudden, wasn't it?"

"Her heart give out."

"Well, the poor thing, and she was such a love." I wondered if I'd laid it on too thick. Justine was staring at me like I'd come to the wrong place. "Would you happen to know if she got my last note?" I asked.

"I wouldn't know anything about that."

"Because I wasn't sure what to do about the money."

"She owed you money?"

"No, no. I owed *her* … which is why I wrote."

Justine hesitated. "How much?"

"Well, it wasn't much," I said, with embarrassment. "Six hundred dollars, but she was such a doll to lend it to me and then I felt so bad when I couldn't pay her back right away. I asked her if I could wait and pay her this month, but then I never heard. Now I don't know what to do."

I could sense the shift in her attitude. Greed seems to do that in record time. "You could pay it to me and I could see it went into her estate," she said helpfully.

"Oh, I don't want to put you to any trouble."

"I don't mind," she said. "You want to come in?"

"I shouldn't. You're probably busy and you've already been so nice …"

"I can take a few minutes."

"Well. If you're sure," I said.

Justine held the door open and I stepped into the trailer, where I got my first clear look at her. This girl was probably thirty pounds overweight with listless brown hair pulled into an oily ponytail. Like Sis, she was decked out in a pair of jeans, with an oversize T-shirt hanging almost to her knees. It was clear big butts ran in the family. She shoved some junk aside so I could sit down on the banquette, a fancy word for the ripped plastic seat that extended along one wall in the kitchenette.

"Did she suffer much?" I asked.

"Doctor said not. He said it was quick, as far as he could tell. Her heart probably seized up and she fell down dead before she could draw a breath."

"It must have been just terrible for you."

Her cheeks flushed with guilt. "You know, her and me had a falling out."

"Really? Well, I'm sorry to hear that. Of course, she always said you two had your differences. I hope it wasn't anything serious."

"She drank. I begged her and begged her to give it up, but she wouldn't pay me no mind," Justine said.

"Did she 'go' here at home?"

She shook her head. "In a welfare hotel. Down on her luck. Drink had done her in. If only I'd known … if only she'd reached out."

I thought she was going to weep, but she couldn't quite manage it. I clutched her hand. "She was too proud," I said.

"I guess that's what it was. I've been thinking to make some kind of contribution to AA, or something like that. You know, in her name."

"A Marge Crispin Memorial Fund," I suggested.

"Like that, yes. I was thinking this money you're talking about might be a start."

"That's a beautiful thought. I'm going right out to the car for my chequebook so I can write you a cheque."

It was a relief to get out into the fresh air again. I'd never heard so much horsepuckey in all my life. Still, it hardly constituted proof she was a murderess.

I hopped in my car and headed for a pay phone, spotting one in a gas station half a block away. I pulled change out of the bottom of my handbag and dialed Sis Dunaway's motel room. She was not very happy to hear my report.

"You didn't find anything?" she said. "Are you positive?"

"Well, of course I'm not positive. All I'm saying is that so far, there's no evidence that anything's amiss. If Justine contributed to her mother's death, she was damned clever about it. I gather the autopsy didn't show a thing."

"Maybe it was some kind of poison that leaves no trace."

"Uh, Sis? I hate to tell you this, but there really isn't such a poison that I ever heard of. I know it's a common fantasy, but there's just no such thing."

Her tone turned stubborn. "But it's possible. You have to admit that. There could be such a thing. It might be from South America … darkest Africa, someplace like that."

Oh, boy. We were really tripping out on this one. I squinted at the receiver. "How would Justine acquire the stuff?"

"How do I know? I'm not going to set here and solve the whole case for you! You're the one gets paid thirty dollars an hour, not me."

"Do you want me to pursue it?"

"Not if you mean to charge me an arm and a leg!" she said. "Listen here, I'll pay sixty dollars more, but you better come up with something or I want my money back."

She hung up before I could protest. How could she get her money back when she hadn't paid this portion? I stood in the phone booth and thought about things. In spite of myself, I'll admit I was hooked. Sis Dunaway might harbour a lot of foolish ideas, but her conviction was unshakable. Add to that the fact that Justine was lying about *something* and you have the kind of situation I can't walk away from.

I drove back to the trailer park and eased my car into a shady spot just across the street. Within moments, Justine appeared in a banged-up white Pinto, trailing smoke out of the tail pipe. Following her wasn't hard. I just hung my nose out the window and kept an eye on the haze. She drove over to Milagro Street to the branch office of a savings and loan. I pulled into a parking spot a few doors down and followed her in, keeping well out of sight. She was dealing with the branch manager, who eventually walked her over to a teller and authorized the cashing of a quite large cheque, judging from the number of bills the teller counted out.

Justine departed moments later, clutching her handbag protectively. I would have been willing to bet she'd been cashing that insurance cheque. She drove back to the trailer where she made a brief stop, probably to drop the money off.

She got back in her car and drove out of the trailer park. I followed discreetly as she headed into town. She pulled into a public parking lot and I eased in after her, finding an empty slot far enough away to disguise my purposes. So far, she didn't seem to have any idea she was being tailed. I kept my distance as she cut through to State Street and walked up a block to Santa Teresa Travel. I pretended to peruse the posters in the window while I watched her chat with the travel agent sitting at a desk just inside the front door. The two transacted business, the agent handing over what apparently were prearranged tickets. Justine wrote out a cheque. I busied myself at a newspaper rack, extracting a paper as she came out again. She walked down State Street half a block to a hobby shop where she purchased one of life's ugliest plastic floral wreaths. Busy little lady, this one, I thought.

She emerged from the hobby shop and headed down a side street, moving into the front entrance of a beauty salon. A surreptitious glance through the window showed her, moments later, in a green plastic cape, having a long conversation with the stylist about a cut. I checked my watch. It was almost twelve-thirty. I scooted back to the travel agency and waited until I saw Justine's travel agent leave the premises for lunch. As soon as she was out of sight, I went in, glancing at the nameplate on the edge of her desk.

The blond agent across the aisle caught my eye and smiled.

"What happened to Kathleen?" I asked.

"She went out to lunch. You just missed her. Is there something I can help you with?"

"Gee, I hope so. I picked up some tickets a little while ago and now I can't find the itinerary she tucked in the envelope. Is there any way you could run me a copy real quick? I'm in a hurry and I really can't afford to wait until she gets back."

"Sure, no problem. What's the name?"

"Justine Crispin," I said.

I found the nearest public phone and dialed Sis's motel room again. "Catch this," I said. "At four o'clock, Justine takes off for Los Angeles. From there, she flies to Mexico City."

"Well, that little shit."

"It gets worse. It's one-way."

"I knew it! I just knew she was up to no good. Where is she now?"

"Getting her hair done. She went to the bank first and cashed a big cheque—"

"I bet it was the insurance."

"That'd be my guess."

"She's got all that money *on* her?"

"Well, no. She stopped by the trailer first and then went and picked up her plane ticket. I think she intends to stop by the cemetery and put a wreath on Marge's grave...."

"I can't stand this. I just can't stand it. She's going to take all that money and make a mockery of Marge's death."

"Hey, Sis, come on. If Justine's listed as the beneficiary, there's nothing you can do."

"That's what you think. I'll make her pay for this, I swear to God I will!" Sis slammed the phone down.

I could feel my heart sink. Uh-oh. I tried to think whether I'd mentioned the name of the beauty salon. I had visions of Sis descending on Justine with a tommy gun. I loitered uneasily outside the shop, watching traffic in both directions. There was no sign of Sis. Maybe she was going to wait until Justine went out to the gravesite before she mowed her down.

At two-fifteen, Justine came out of the beauty shop and passed me on the street. She was nearly unrecognizable. Her hair had been cut and permed and it fell in soft curls around her freshly made-up face. The beautician had found ways to bring out her eyes, subtly heightening her colouring with a touch of blusher on her cheeks. She looked like a million bucks—or a hundred thousand, at any rate. She was in a jaunty mood, paying more attention to her own reflection in the passing store windows than she was to me, hovering half a block behind.

She returned to the parking lot and retrieved her Pinto, easing into the flow of traffic as it moved up State. I tucked in a few cars back, all the while scanning for some sign of Sis. I couldn't imagine what she'd try to do, but as mad as she was, I had to guess she had some scheme in the works.

Fifteen minutes later, we were turning into the trailer park, Justine leading while I lollygagged along behind. I had already used up the money Sis had authorized, but by this time I had my own stake in the outcome. For all I knew, I was going to end up protecting Justine from an assassination attempt. She stopped by the trailer just long enough to load her bags in the car and then she drove out to the Santa Teresa Memorial Park, which was out by the airport.

The cemetery was deserted, a sunny field of gravestones among flowering shrubs. When the road forked, I watched Justine wind up the lane to the right while I headed left, keeping an eye on her car, which I could see across a wide patch of grass. She parked and got out, carrying the wreath to an oblong depression in the ground where a temporary marker had been set, awaiting the permanent monument. She rested the wreath against the marker and stood there looking down. She seemed awfully exposed and I couldn't help but wish she'd duck down some to grieve. Sis was probably crouched somewhere with a knife between her teeth, ready to leap out and stab Justine in the neck.

Respects paid, Justine got back into her car and drove to the airport where she checked in for her flight. By now, I was feeling baffled. She had less than an hour before the plane was scheduled to depart and there was still no sign of Sis. If there was going to be a showdown, it was bound to happen soon. I ambled into the gift shop and inserted myself between the wall and a book rack, watching Justine through windows nearly obscured by a display of Santa Teresa T-shirts. She sat on a bench and calmly read a paperback.

What was going on here?

Sis Dunaway had seemed hell-bent on avenging Marge's death, but where was she? Had she gone to the cops? I kept one eye on the clock and one eye on Justine. Whatever Sis was up to, she had better do it quick. Finally, mere minutes before the flight was due to be called, I left the newsstand, crossed the gate area, and took a seat beside Justine. "Hi," I said. "Nice permanent. Looks good."

She glanced at me and then did a classic double take. "What are you doing here?"

"Keeping an eye on you."

"What for?"

"I thought someone should see you off. I suspect your Aunt Sis is en route, so I decided to keep you company until she gets here."

"Aunt *Sis*?" she said, incredulously.

"I gotta warn you, she's not convinced your mother had a heart attack."

"What are you talking about? Aunt Sis is dead."

I could feel myself smirk. "Yeah, sure. Since when?"

"Five years ago."

"Bullshit."

"It's not bullshit. An aneurysm burst and she dropped in her tracks."

"Come on," I scoffed.

"It's the truth," she said emphatically. By that time, she'd recovered her composure and she went on the offensive. "Where's my money? You said you'd write a cheque for six hundred bucks."

"Completely dead?" I asked.

The loudspeaker came on. "May I have your attention, please. United Flight 3440 for Los Angeles is now ready for boarding at Gate Five. Please have your boarding pass available and prepare for security check."

Justine began to gather up her belongings. I'd been wondering how she was going to get all that cash through the security checkpoint, but one look at her lumpy waistline and it was obvious she'd strapped on a money belt. She picked up her carry-on, her shoulder bag, her jacket, and her paperback and clopped, in spike heels, over to the line of waiting passengers.

I followed, befuddled, reviewing the entire sequence of events. It had all happened today. Within hours. It wasn't like I was suffering brain damage or memory loss. And I hadn't seen a ghost. Sis had come to my office and laid out the whole tale about Marge and Justine. She'd told me all about their relationship, Justine's history as a con, the way the two women tried to outdo each other, the insurance, Marge's death. How could a murder have gotten past Dr. Yee? Unless the woman wasn't murdered, I thought suddenly.

Oh.

Once I saw it in *that* light, it was obvious.

Justine got in line between a young man with a duffel bag and a woman toting a cranky baby. There was some delay up ahead while the ticket agent got set. The line started to move and Justine advanced a step with me right beside her.

"I understand you and your mother had quite a competitive relationship."

"What's it to you," she said. She kept her eyes averted, facing dead ahead, willing the line to move so she could get away from me.

"I understand you were always trying to get the better of each other."

"What's your point?" she said, annoyed.

I shrugged. "I figure you read the article about the unidentified dead woman in the welfare hotel. You went out to the morgue and claimed the body as your mom's. The two of you agreed to split the insurance money, but your mother got worried about a double cross, which is exactly what this is."

"You don't know what you're talking about."

The line moved up again and I stayed right next to her. "She hired me to keep an eye on you, so when I realized you were leaving town, I called her and told her what was going on. She really hit the roof and I thought she'd charge right out, but so far there's been no sign of her...."

Justine showed her ticket to the agent and he motioned her on. She moved through the metal detector without setting it off.

I gave the agent a smile. "Saying good-bye to a friend," I said, and passed through the wooden arch right after she did. She was picking up the pace, anxious to reach the plane.

I was still talking, nearly jogging to keep up with her. "I couldn't figure out why she wasn't trying to stop you and then I realized what she must have done—"

"Get away from me. I don't want to talk to you."

"She took the money, Justine. There's probably nothing in the belt but old papers. She had plenty of time to make the switch while you were getting your hair done."

"Ha, ha," she said sarcastically. "Tell me another one."

I stopped in my tracks. "All right. That's all I'm gonna say. I just didn't want you to reach Mexico City and find yourself flat broke."

"Blow it out your buns," she hissed. She showed her boarding pass to the woman at the gate and passed on through. I could hear her spike heels tip-tapping out of ear range.

I reversed myself, walked back through the gate area and out to the walled exterior courtyard, where I could see the planes through a windbreak of protective glass. Justine crossed the tarmac to the waiting plane, her shoulders set. I didn't think she'd heard me, but then I saw her hand stray to her waist. She walked a few more steps and then halted, dumping her belongings in a pile at her feet. She pulled her shirt up and checked the money belt. At that distance, I saw her mouth open, but it took a second for the shrieks of outrage to reach me.

Ah, well, I thought. Sometimes a mother's love is like a poison that leaves no trace. You bop along through life, thinking you've got it made, and next thing you know, you're dead.